ALL I'VE WAITED FOR

A WALKER BEACH ROMANCE

LINDSAY HARREL

For my GLAM Girls—
Gabrielle Meyer, Alena Tauriainen, and Melissa Tagg

Thank you for being my people.

CHAPTER 1

*L*ife these days was a never-ending sprint.

Good thing Ashley Baker liked to run.

Her feet pounded the wooden boardwalk and music poured through her AirPods as she wove around people out for a leisurely stroll along the Pacific Ocean's edge. In the distance, seagulls lazily dipped toward the water. Neighborhood children built sandcastles, their parents watching from the shade of a nearby umbrella. The seventy-degree sun and clear skies had lured townspeople of all generations out to enjoy this late-April Saturday in Walker Beach, California, the small town nestled off Highway 1 between Los Angeles and San Francisco where Ashley had lived her entire life.

How tempting it was to join them.

But Kyle Mahaney, her boss, would kill Ashley if she arrived late to their new clients' meeting at Whimsical Weddings & More. He'd even asked her to come a few minutes earlier than usual, which had meant cutting short the planning meeting for this summer's Baker family reunion. Thankfully it only took seven and a half minutes to jog from her parents' house to the downtown office.

Ashley's music halted as a call came through her phone, which was tucked in the back pocket of her jeans. Slowing to a brisk walk, she answered the call. "Ashley here."

"Hey, cuz."

"Hi." Normally, she'd love to chat with Shannon. But not right now. "Sorry, I only have like two seconds."

"So what's new?" An easy laugh filled the line, and Ashley pictured her cousin's bright eyes and winsome smile. They looked more like sisters than cousins, both tan with long blonde hair—although at nearly six feet, Ashley stood a half-foot taller. And, while Ashley's build was more athletic in nature, Shannon's delicate features matched her artistic spirit well. "You're always busy."

"Yeah, yeah." What could she say? Ashley loved planning events and she loved people, so when there was a chance to volunteer for something events related, she almost always said yes.

Staying busy also had the happy advantage of keeping her mind off of less pleasant things.

The sea lapped along the shore, sparkling under the midday Californian sun. "So, what's up?"

"Just wondering if you'd seen him yet."

Ashley nearly groaned at the reminder. "He's only been back in town for a day."

Stepping off the boardwalk, she took the intersecting sidewalk to Main Street in the North Village. This part of town had experienced damage from an earthquake nine months ago, and some businesses had never recovered. Thankfully, Kyle's business hadn't been one of them, and Ashley's job had remained secure.

"What's he waiting for? Your house should've been his first stop."

"I don't think anyone else has seen him either." Ashley only knew Derek Campbell was back because earlier this week his dad, Jack, had informed her of his impending return. The thought still tightened her throat. "Haven't heard anything from the Walker Beach gossips, anyway."

"But you're going to tell him how you feel when you see him, right?"

"It's been over a year since he left. Things are bound to be different between us."

"No way. You guys had something special even though neither of you ever said anything."

A sigh filtered across the airwaves. With all of Shannon's romantic notions, it was a wonder that she'd never had a boyfriend. Probably had something to do with feeling stuck in her older sister Quinn's shadow—and her extreme shyness when it came to any male their age that she wasn't related to.

"You deserve to be happy, Ash. Just promise me you'll think about it, okay?"

Shannon was never pushy. This obviously meant a lot to her.

"Okay, okay. *If* he ever comes to see me." Ashley flitted past a few shoppers and finally reached the pale pink storefront where she worked. The front window display—which Shannon had helped design a year ago when Ashley had started her job here—showed off a lovely A-line wedding dress with see-through sleeves and intricate beading on the bodice. A ladder shelf created a pretty hodgepodge of wedding-themed elements, from a large wooden Mr. & Mrs. to hurricane vases, soft pink candles, and paper lanterns. "Sorry, Shan, I've gotta go. I'll see you tomorrow night at Family Dinner, right?"

"Of course. I'd never risk the wrath of the Baker Matrons."

Ashley laughed in response as she opened the door and a bell rang overhead. "I always knew you were smart."

They said goodbye and Ashley strode through the small showroom that exhibited scrapbooks, sample wedding invitations, and a whole wall of framed photos featuring gorgeous brides of all shapes and colors with one thing in common—their faces shone with love.

And each one had a man who loved them back.

She turned her head and kept walking until she reached Kyle's office in the back. "Knock, knock."

Her boss looked up from his tidy desk. "Ah, come in, Ashley, come in." The room smelled of coconut, probably from the sunscreen Kyle wore religiously ever since his wife, Cathy, had died of skin cancer ten years ago.

"I hope I'm not late." She slid into the overstuffed chair on the other side of the desk, sinking into the plush maroon cushions. Her muscles relaxed even if her brain couldn't. Kyle hadn't said why he wanted to meet early. Ashley had wracked her brain all day trying to think of something she'd missed, but other than a minor miscommunication with one of their brides that Kyle had cleaned up, she couldn't think of anything.

"No, we have a few minutes until our appointment." Kyle leaned back in his chair and fiddled with the end of his white handlebar mustache. With his Harley-Davidson jean vest, cowboy hat covering a bald head, and wide girth, he was the very opposite of what one would picture as a wedding planner. But this business had been his wife's dream, and when she'd passed, he'd quit his job as a trucker and taken up her mantle, whipping up some of the most fabulous events Walker Beach had ever seen.

"Great. So, what did you want to talk about?" Ashley crossed her legs, then uncrossed them again.

"The future." Kyle sighed. "I'm getting older, and as you know, the pace of this business can be stressful. Hiring you on has helped tremendously, but I've found myself more and more ready for a rest."

Ashley released a whoosh of air. Nothing she'd done wrong, then. "I understand needing a vacation." Kyle always seemed to have everything well in hand, but she really wasn't surprised by his stress level given his business's success and the way he held tight to the reins—even those he'd given Ashley charge over. "Are you planning to go soon? I can handle the Whitman wedding and the Dreyfuss anniversary party on my own, no problem."

"No, Ashley. What I'm saying is that I've decided to retire."

"What? When?"

"In about two months. Late June sometime."

"I see." Her days wouldn't be the same without him here. Kyle could be gruff at times, and he expected a lot from her, but really he was just a big softie underneath all that bluster.

But wait. What was she thinking? This was *his* company. "What's going to happen to the business?" Was she about to be out of a job?

Or maybe ... maybe the chance to live out her childhood dreams was finally here.

For years, Ashley had wanted to start her own wedding planning business. After getting a bachelor's in event management online while busing tables at Froggies—her aunt and uncle's pizza parlor and arcade—she'd worked as an assistant event planner for the city of Walker Beach. A great experience, but she'd always longed to focus on weddings. So when Kyle had opened a position at Whimsical Weddings, she'd jumped at the chance and had loved every minute there.

Sure, she'd do some things differently than he did, and yes, she wished Kyle would trust her to handle some weddings by herself. But the chance to help brides have the most perfect day ever ... well, that was right up Ashley's alley. This job had been a fabulous jumping-off point for that. Yet still her desire lingered, tucked away in the corner of her heart for some time in the future when she had the time, energy, and money to devote to it.

But maybe "the future" was now.

Ashley leaned forward in anticipation of Kyle's response.

He scratched his chin and looked away from her, studying the potted succulent in the corner of the room. It had started blooming since she'd last been in here, its baby pink flowers barely open. Ashley had given it to Kyle on the last anniversary of his wife's death.

"Cathy started this company thirty years ago, you know. She built it from the ground up, and it meant the world to her." His voice always went soft when he spoke of his wife.

"I know." Cathy, who had been friends with her parents, was one of the kindest, gentlest souls Ashley had ever met.

"She always talked about leaving the business to our children, but ..." Kyle cleared his throat.

Somehow, she remembered overhearing Cathy and Mom talking on the couch one day when Ashley was about ten. Cathy had cried and cried over yet another failed adoption.

Now, Ashley resisted the urge to cross the room and hug Kyle. Her boss probably wouldn't appreciate the sympathy, which he would undoubtedly interpret as pity. "What's your plan, then?" They may not be related by blood, but Kyle was a mentor to her, someone she trusted to steer her in the right direction in more than just business, and she'd like to think he thought of her as a kind of daughter—or at the very least, as a friend.

Were they on the same page? Was Kyle going to leave her the business?

Ashley gripped the sides of her chair, her stomach fluttering.

"I have a niece in San Francisco. She's always been interested in event planning. Even interned with us several years back."

The words punched Ashley in the gut. "Oh." It was a miracle she could get the response past her lips.

"Are you all right? You look pale."

"I'm fine." What could she say? He had every right to do what he wanted with his business. "So, you've asked her then? She wants to move here and take it over?"

Frowning, he lifted the hat off his head and fanned himself. "Not yet, no. But I plan to go up and see my sister tomorrow, and her daughter will be there. Thought it better to talk about in person."

So Ashley still had a shot—but should she take it? Cathy had wanted to keep the business in the family, and Ashley should respect that. She'd just let it go. "I hope the conversation goes well."

Kyle's hawk eyes studied her. "And if she doesn't want it, well …"

Ashley's gaze collided with his. "You aren't going to close the business, are you?" He couldn't, wouldn't, not when it had meant so much to Cathy.

Not when it meant so much to Ashley—the chance it represented, anyway.

"I don't know that I have a choice." Kyle folded his hands over his stomach. "Not unless …"

Somehow Ashley had scooted to the front edge of her seat. "Unless what?"

"Unless there was someone else who wanted it."

"Yes!" Ashley felt her eyes widen at the intensity of her declaration and she clapped a hand over her mouth.

Kyle chuckled. "So you might be interested in buying me out?"

Her chest deflated. "I don't have the funds to do that." Maybe she could get a business loan, though. Something. "But if you give me a chance to look into it, I'd be interested." She paused. "Very interested. It … it would be a dream, actually."

"Is this some whim or something you've thought about before?"

"I never really thought about taking over your business, necessarily. I've been content to just learn from you. But yes, I've wanted to own a wedding planning business since I can remember." Ashley placed a hand flat on the desk. "And I'd be honored to continue Cathy's legacy, even if I'm not a Mahaney."

"I believe you would." Back and forth Kyle swiveled ever so slightly in his desk chair, the wheels emitting a low squeak. "And regarding the money, I'd be fine with a slow purchase. You could pay me over the course of five years, or maybe we'd go into it as partners—you doing the labor, and me as an investor of sorts, until your portion was paid."

What a kind man. What an opportunity. "That is so generous."

Kyle's eyes narrowed a bit. "It's still business. With this solution, I'd actually be paid for the business, which is more than I'd get if I left it to my niece."

"Of course." Ashley bit her lip to hold back a grin. The teddy bear was hiding behind the grizzly's teeth, but she knew better.

"I'm serious, young lady." Kyle tilted his head. "The money isn't a concern to me, but the legacy part is. And I do have some concerns about your ability to handle it."

Really? Ashley had been nothing but helpful and competent. She couldn't help but feel the nip of his words. "In what way?"

"Your level of experience, for one. And your schedule for another. You're busy all the time."

"So are you."

"Yes, but mine is mostly business related. You're always running from one meeting to another. First, you were on the library board—"

"Which I've stepped down from." Her friend Madison had recently taken over as Walker Beach's head librarian, so Ashley hadn't felt the town needed her as much anymore.

"Yes, but what else have you added? You're overseeing the town's committee for the Christmas festival—"

"The community development officer personally asked if I'd do that. And the whole idea of the festival is for the town to band together and revitalize our economy after the earthquake harmed it."

"I know, Ashley. I'm on the committee too, remember?"

"Right." She shouldn't get so defensive.

"And aren't you also coordinating your family's reunion this summer? Not to mention taking on extra responsibilities and saying yes to everyone who asks something of you. Cumulatively, it's a lot, and adding the ownership of a business might be too much. You're used to having my help with every event, and you've had me to fall back on when you weren't sure about something. But if I retire and it's all on your shoulders ... well, I don't want you to flounder."

He didn't believe she could do this? "I don't want that either."

"Your heart is in the right place. I just want to be sure you can actually handle this before you've got money invested and Cathy's legacy is put in danger."

"I'd never want that either." Ashley furrowed her brow. "How can I prove to you that I've got this?"

The bell jangled from the showroom.

Kyle glanced at the clock on the wall. "It's about time for our appointment. We'll have to continue this conversation later." He gathered his planner, then paused. His lips twisted to the side. "You know, this couple has asked for a very quick turnaround. They want to be married Memorial Day weekend."

Ashley's jaw fell. "That's only six weeks away."

"I know, but they were desperate and didn't blink at the premium I quoted for the rush. And Moonstone Lodge happens to be available on the date in question."

"Wow, really?" She straightened. Where was he going with this? "Okay."

"You asked how you can prove yourself to me. Take on this wedding all by yourself. I'll stay completely out of it. You run the show. If you can pull it off with everything else you have going on, you'll demonstrate that this is important enough to

9

you. We'll work out the other ownership details later if it goes well. How does that sound?"

Ashley squealed and leaped from her seat, rounding the desk and throwing her arms around Kyle's neck. "I say you've got yourself a deal."

"Settle down or our clients will think we're hiding a pig back here."

Laughing, Ashley kissed him on the cheek and stole his planner from him. "I'll take that. You just stay here and relax. Or better yet, go out and enjoy the sunshine."

"Maybe I will."

With pep in her step, Ashley closed his door behind her and paused, adrenaline working its way through her whole system. As she entered the showroom, she caught sight of a tall brunette perusing the photo wall. The woman looked up, and Ashley was struck by her large blue eyes.

She held out her hand. "Hi, there. I'm Ashley Baker, your wedding planner."

The woman, who wore a couture black-and-white tie-neck blouse and pencil skirt, returned her shake. "Claire Boivin. My fiancé will be here in a moment. He's parking the car."

"You have a lovely accent." Ashley smiled warmly. "Do you live nearby?"

"*Non*, I'm from France. My fiancé lives here, though." Claire arched an eyebrow. "I believe I spoke with a man on the phone, *oui*?" She walked toward the silk flower display and began flipping through the book of photos.

From her movements to her dainty nose, thin lips, and smooth pale skin, this woman oozed elegance and grace. In Ashley's experience, brides like her were typically high maintenance with unrealistic expectations, but that didn't fit with someone whose planning timetable was so short. Or Ashley hoped so, anyway. It would be challenging enough to pull together something small and simple, but if the woman desired a blowout bash, well … Ashley wasn't going to sleep for the next six weeks.

Still, it would be worth it to finally own the business of her dreams.

She followed Claire to the display. "Yes, that was my boss, Kyle. He's appointed me as the lead planner, and I'm very excited to make your dreams come true."

Claire nodded, apparently satisfied.

They both turned as the bell chimed. Ashley's eyes widened at the tall man with broad shoulders who entered.

Derek had finally come to see her.

She rushed toward him, trying to still her shaking hands. Oh man, he looked good, better than she remembered. His brown hair was swept back in an Elvis cut, and his skin had bronzed, probably from so much time in the French vineyards. He'd grown a beard, and though Ashley wasn't normally one for facial hair, it suited him.

"Hi. It's so good to see you." She lowered her voice. "I'm with a client right now, but I'd love to catch up. Can I meet you for coffee in about an hour?"

Derek stared at Ashley as if he'd never seen her before, his deep brown eyes crinkling at the corners. "Ashley? What are you doing here?"

As if he'd slapped her, she took a step back. "What do you m—"

"Derek? Do you two know each other?"

Ashley froze. Her eyes moved from Derek to Claire, blinking rapidly. Understanding dawned as Claire joined them, each click of her heels on tile punctuating the truth.

Derek wasn't here to see Ashley.

Well, he was. Just not in the way she'd dreamed about.

"You're …" She cleared her throat. "You're the groom?"

He averted his eyes, swinging his head toward Claire, who smiled at him. "I am."

No. No, no, no.

Ashley forced a smile. "Would you excuse me for a moment?" Then she turned and bolted toward the back as gracefully as she could.

Kyle would have to take this wedding. She couldn't do it.

Reaching for the doorknob, she twisted it, but her hand was too slick with sweat to get it the first time. Finally, she managed to open the door.

Kyle didn't glance up from the bridal magazine he was reading. "Did our experiment fail already?" He licked his finger and turned the page.

Ashley grimaced. What was she doing in here? She couldn't give up her dream opportunity. Not over a guy who hadn't bothered to call one of his supposed best friends more than once after he'd gone overseas fourteen months ago.

Over someone who had gotten engaged and hadn't bothered to let her know.

"Not at all." Her gaze tumbled over Kyle's desk until she caught sight of a random checklist. Ashley swooped in and grabbed it. "Just needed this."

Without waiting to gauge Kyle's reaction, she left the office as quickly as she'd come in.

Before she entered the showroom again, she stopped and took a deep breath. Yeah, this was going to be awkward, but she could do it. She'd likely be working mostly with Claire anyway, and she'd just try to forget that Derek was the groom.

Try to forget how, despite his distance and the way he'd acted like their friendship—like she—meant nothing to him, Ashley Baker was still in love with him.

Oh boy.

She steeled her spine and walked into the room. "All right, ya'll, let's get this wedding planned!"

~

Things were much worse than he'd thought.

Derek Campbell leaned forward in the wooden Adirondack chair on his family home's multilevel deck. "What time does Jorge get in on Monday? I've got some ideas I'd like to discuss about the day-to-day operations."

"Let's talk about that later. You just got home, and I want to get to know your lovely fiancée better." His father's hand shook slightly as he lifted a glass of Campbell Wines' 2017 Syrah to his lips and sipped. The fifty-eight-year-old had thinned considerably since Derek had left for France, and the yellow ringing his eyes was undeniable proof that his stage 4 kidney disease had fought hard in Derek's absence.

Beside Dad, Derek's stepmother, Nancy, watched him with pinched lips. She was worried about something and trying not to show it. From what Derek had seen in the last twenty-four hours, she had every right to be concerned on multiple fronts.

But Derek was here now, and he was going to fix this. For all of them.

Dad turned toward Claire, who sat in a chair next to Derek, sipping her glass of 2019 rosé as she looked out across the expansive vineyard before them. From here, he could hardly make out the light from the row of rental cabins to the east, one of which he was calling home for the time being. The others had been out of commission for a few years. "Now that you've had a chance to see our little town and home, what do you think? How does it compare with yours?"

The evening sun was on the cusp of setting behind them, spilling gold and orange across the rows and rows of grapes. Even though they were only five miles outside of Walker Beach, the vineyard felt like another world, tucked away against the foothills and trees that lined one side of the town.

Most would say nothing compared to the lush green of the Loire Valley in France, but this … this was home. And Derek would do anything necessary to protect it. For all of them, but mostly for Dad. This place meant everything to him.

Claire twiddled her thumb against the rim of her glass. "It is much the same, except everyone here speaks English, of course."

Nancy crossed her legs and tilted her head. "Now, Claire, forgive me for saying so, but you don't strike me as a small-town girl—not unless all French women are as poised and well styled as you." Nancy herself stuck to mostly jeans and flannel, and she lacked the same charm he admired in Claire, but she was nice enough. She'd made his dad happy for the last five years, anyway, and they seemed to love each other.

For now. Hopefully she wouldn't leave when things got even rougher, though Derek wouldn't be all that surprised if she did.

From what Derek had seen, love was a fickle mistress.

Claire smoothed the front of her skirt and smiled. "*Non*, we are as varied as you Americans. But I did grow up in the city."

"Oh?" Dad wheezed, and held up a hand toward Nancy before she could ask if he was okay. The episode passed, and they all breathed better. He continued. "Then how did you two meet?"

Claire eyed Derek. If she were worried that Derek hadn't told his family much about her—okay, nothing actually, other than the fact he was engaged and bringing his fiancée home for a bit—she didn't show it. "My grandfather owns the vineyard where Derek interned. I lived with my mother in Paris as a child and visited the vineyard every summer. Fell in love with it immediately. It is a part of me. I believe you understand this." She tilted a smile at Dad.

He grinned back. "I do indeed."

"*Oui.* A few years ago, I decided to work for my grandfather full time. He is getting older, having some memory issues. While he would not admit it, he needed my help. And I was glad to give it, to gain the chance to learn more about the operational side of the business. You see, I'm set to inherit the vineyard when ..." Claire placed her wineglass on the low wooden table that separated her and Derek from his dad and Nancy, then casually sneaked her hand inside of Derek's. "Well, eventually."

"And that's how we met." Derek checked his watch. They had a lot to discuss, and today had been a waste of time.

Okay, *waste* was probably too strong of a word, given that he'd been able to catch up with his sisters, niece, dad, and stepmom. But other than his and Claire's appointment to start planning their wedding this afternoon, nothing they'd done had moved him any closer to his goal.

And it was questionable whether the appointment had really done so. He'd hardly heard a word of it—not when he'd seen *her* again.

Ashley Baker had always been a knockout, but today she'd been positively radiant in her tight jeans, a red shirt that brought out the blue in her eyes, and that blonde hair hanging to her trim waist. But the way his breath had caught at the sight of her had nothing to do with her looks.

Okay, maybe not *nothing*. But it was much more driven by the very real reminder of the way she'd splayed open his heart with her rejection all those months ago.

Still, despite the memories, Derek had to stay focused on the reason he'd returned to Walker Beach in the first place. And even if it were a bit uncomfortable, he would work with Ashley and Claire to get a nice wedding planned. Claire deserved that and more.

He fixed his gaze on Dad again, who looked ready to bend in half and take a snooze. "So ... Jorge?"

Nancy gave Dad that look once more, patted his arm, and stood. "Claire, you look as tired as I feel. Would you like to head inside with me?"

Claire squeezed Derek's hand. "Of course." She leaned over and kissed his cheek, the scent of her vanilla perfume enveloping him, then followed Nancy into the two-story house.

15

He turned. "Is everything all right, Dad?"

His father set aside his glass and stood, nearly toppling over at the movement.

Derek jumped forward to help him, but Dad swatted his hand away. "I'm fine, son." Picking up his cane, he pointed it toward the field. "Let's walk and talk."

Jack Campbell was a stubborn man, and Derek had always admired him for it. But right now, with his health clearly failing, Derek couldn't help but wish his father had a little less bull and a little more sheep in him.

They made their way down the wooden deck steps and onto the dirt and soil. With his dad next to him, they made slow progress. Derek examined the nearest plant, finding tiny green buds and miniature grape leaves sprouting along the vine. Their shoots grew upward as their workers had been instructed to prune any down-facing shoots. This practice reduced the number of overall grapes they'd get, but that didn't worry Derek. Any viticulturist worth his salt knew that allowing the vine to focus on fewer grapes led to a more concentrated product, and he'd much rather have quality over quantity.

"How are the vines doing as a whole this year?" They'd talked about business here and there while he was overseas, but Dad had always seemed to change the subject somehow.

Now, he remained quiet for a few long moments, his lips quirked to one side. "We lost some in the eastern quadrant to disease last month."

That stopped Derek in his tracks. "How did Jorge let that happen?" The vineyard manager should have had his people checking the plants religiously every week. There was no excuse for that. "What are we paying him for?"

"We're not."

"Come again?"

His dad sighed and leaned heavily on his cane. "I had to let him go four months ago."

"What?" Derek couldn't help the bite in his tone. "Why?"

"You know I purchased new equipment a few years back. Then I was in the hospital for a short spell last year. The bills started adding up. I had to make a tough call."

And Derek's sisters hadn't told him? He was going to be having a very frank discussion with them both, and soon. "I would have come home."

"Which is exactly why I didn't tell you. Your purpose in going to France was to learn new ways of doing things, to bring our vineyard up to snuff, make us more competitive."

"But that will only work if the vineyard is still around long enough for me to implement what I've learned." Derek dragged his hands through his hair. "What about that grant you received from the city of Walker Beach a few months ago?"

"It's significant, but I'm not sure it'll be enough, not since the hospital bills hit. Our insurance is only for catastrophic stuff." Dad looked out across the field, quiet. He'd once been the strongest man Derek knew, someone who ruled his house and business with wisdom and kindness, but also an iron will. *Now look at him.*

His gut twisted. "Did you look into a business loan?"

The sad smile on Dad's face let Derek know his father was one step ahead of him. "Banks won't lend to people who are in debt as far as I am."

Thank goodness Derek had a solution to all of this, then. He only wished he'd been able to spare his dad for the last four months. It must have been difficult to let Jorge go, to hire someone less proficient. The man had been at Campbell Wines for nearly twenty-five years.

"So who's been doing Jorge's job then?" Both his sisters worked at the winery—Christina as its marketing manager and Heather as the wine shop manager—but neither of them had much experience in the field. That had always been Derek's expertise. From an early age, he'd been groomed to take over the family business, just like five generations of Campbell men before him. "Did you hire someone externally or promote Greg?"

"Neither." Dad started walking again, the clatter of his cane softened by the dirt. "I've been doing it."

Biting back a groan, Derek took two steps and caught up with his father. "No offense, Dad, but your health—"

"I've done what was needed, son. But I must confess, I'm glad to have you home." He turned toward Derek, and even in the fading light, his eyes looked tired.

Derek's throat clogged, and he swallowed hard. "I'm glad to be home."

Considering they'd only been engaged for such a short time, he and Claire hadn't had time to discuss where they would live once they were married. Upon their marriage, she'd inherit her grandfather's vineyard. And when Derek's dad passed ... but his last prognosis had been ten years so long as the disease didn't progress into stage 5.

And who knew? He might get high enough on the transplant list that Derek wouldn't have to worry about splitting his time between here and France for a long, long time. He prayed that was the case.

But first, Derek had to save the vineyard or it would all be a moot point.

"And your fiancée seems to be a lovely person. Beautiful too."

"She is." When he'd arrived at Chateau de Boivin, Derek had been determined to keep his ear to the ground and learn all he could about different ways to run a vineyard—and do all he could to forget the raw ache of leaving home.

Of leaving *her*.

But Ashley hadn't loved him the way he'd loved her, plain and simple. And so he'd done what he needed to move on— flown over five thousand miles around the world.

He hadn't expected to find a companion in Claire.

"How long have you two been an item?"

"I don't know." Derek kicked a rock, and it skidded under the row of plants beside him. "It came on gradually, I guess." During the long days and nights working together, they'd formed a friendship, bonding as they both nursed wounded hearts—though Claire's grief had been much more serious thanks to a broken engagement in her past.

Mutual respect had grown between them, as slow as new shoots on a grapevine. It hadn't even been until a few weeks ago that he'd kissed her in the barrel room. The kiss had been nice, comfortable. Nothing earth rocking, but his world had been rocked once before, and he wasn't anxious to repeat the sensation.

And then last week, when facing his return to the States, she'd suggested that they create a permanent partnership—a way for them to both help their families. And just like that, the solution to the Campbells' problems had lain at Derek's fingertips.

"It's uh … all rather quick, though, isn't it, son?" His dad's cough returned.

Derek waited until Dad stopped wheezing. "I guess so. But when you know something's right, you just know." And this marriage, while unconventional to some, had *right* written all over it. He reversed directions and started back toward the house, his dad following without protest.

"But six weeks? Why the rush?" A spring breeze rustled through the vineyard, and the house came into view once more.

"We're just ready to get married." Dad didn't need to know the particulars. He'd never want Derek to get married to save the vineyard, would want him to be in love. But love couldn't be counted on to last. However, a marriage based on respect, honesty, and mutual benefit—that was something he could get behind.

And thankfully, Claire agreed.

"I would have figured you'd get married in France."

Derek would have considered it, but the whole reason he'd come home from his internship early was because Heather had mentioned Dad's deteriorating health during one of his calls home. And in that moment, he knew they needed him—that it was up to *him* to fix this, just like he'd kept the vineyard going after Mom had left so long ago. "I wanted you to be at the wedding."

His dad huffed. "I can still travel, son. I'm not bedridden."

"But it would be hard for you. No sense in pretending otherwise. It just makes sense to do it here."

"Hmm." The lights of the house appeared on the horizon. "Forgive me for prying, but I always thought your heart tended in a different direction."

He and the whole rest of Walker Beach, apparently. How many times had his buddies ribbed Derek about proclaiming his undying devotion for the woman who'd once upon a time just been his best friend Ben's kid sister—until she wasn't? In fact, the only friend other than Ashley who hadn't seemed to catch on was Ben himself, and Derek hadn't been eager to enlighten him.

"Maybe it did once. But not anymore." It was better this way. Because hearts couldn't be trusted.

Derek's mind, on the other hand, had never failed him yet. And his mind was made up. The way Dad shuffled up the steps with the gait of someone twenty years older only served to strengthen Derek's resolve.

He and Claire would be married two days before Memorial Day—and the fact Ashley Baker was their wedding planner wasn't going to affect him one bit.

Nope. Not one bit.

CHAPTER 2

$\mathcal{W}$ here in the world was Shannon?

From her spot on the couch, Ashley scanned her parents' living room, where Baker upon Baker ate, chatted, laughed, and teased. She'd been here for over an hour with no sign of her cousin—not *that* cousin, anyway. Except for the few who lived out of town, like Shannon's sister Quinn, the majority of Ashley's eleven first cousins on her dad's side were here somewhere, as were her parents, four aunts, three uncles, and one grandma. Between all of them, three little children, and a handful of spouses and significant others, the house held anywhere from thirty to forty people every Sunday night. And that didn't even include the Griffin side of the family.

No wonder the Bakers were considered one of Walker Beach's most prominent families. Not only had the community park and beach been named after Ashley's great-grandfather, but the Bakers themselves would probably take up an entire downtown street block if lined up one after the other.

The air smelled of her Aunt Kiki's manicotti, and the tile floors amplified the din of chatter and scraping forks. Despite the crowd, her mother's modern farmhouse style made for an inviting yet elegant space, and the massive wall of windows facing the backyard made the room appear much larger than it really was.

Normally, Ashley would be hanging out in the kitchen with her mom and aunts, maybe a cousin or two. But she'd chosen this particular spot because the teenage cousin sitting next to Ashley found her phone far more interesting than anything else. Today there was simply too much taking up space in Ashley's brain to put forth the energy to hear what was going on in anyone else's life.

Any small amount of energy she did have was focused on watching for Shannon. Thanks to a corporate brunch she'd overseen this morning, Ashley hadn't had a chance to tell her cousin about any of yesterday's happenings.

Not about Kyle's offer—and definitely not about having Derek as a client.

She polished off her last bite of breadstick, set her plate on the coffee table in front of her, and sank lower into the couch cushions.

"Ashley. There you are." Aunt Jules floated across the room and sat on the arm of the couch next to Ashley. Her long red hair hung in waves down her back, and copper-twisted turquoise bangles swung on her wrists. The scent of her signature lavender perfume wrapped around Ashley, bringing a sense of peace and contentment she couldn't explain. "Are you hiding out over here for any particular reason?"

"What do you mean?"

Jules clucked her tongue. "You're normally the life of the party. What's got you down, Sunshine?" She leaned in closer. "Did you finally get tired of all these biddies asking when you're bringing home a man? Because I hate to inform you—they'll never stop."

Aunt Jules would know. At forty-two, she was the youngest of the five Baker siblings and the only one who remained unmarried. But she never seemed to let it bother her. Besides, as the owner of Serene Art, a hippie art gallery in downtown Walker Beach, she had too much going on to allow her lack of companionship to ruffle her feathers—and Ashley admired her for it. In fact, watching Jules achieve her dreams of owning a business had fueled Ashley's own ambitions. That and the fact her own parents, her brother Ben, and several other family members were also business owners.

Ashley elbowed her aunt's leg. "I'm fine."

Her cousin Sophie's two boys sped through the room wearing capes and eye masks. They ran past Tyler—Shannon's older brother and Quinn's twin—who was chatting with Gabrielle, his wife of seven months, and stuck out their tongues playfully.

"You can't catch us!" the seven-year-old called.

Using his former pro football reflexes, Tyler snapped them both up in his strong arms and growled before unleashing the tickle monster within. After the kids ran off giggling, he turned back to Gabrielle and they shared an intimate grin as he placed a hand on her ever-so-slightly rounded stomach.

What a blessing was coming for them this September. And now that their joint nonprofit work at the Amazing Kids Foundation had brought them back permanently to Walker Beach, Ashley would have a chance to witness it up close.

A tiny twinge of longing wound up and gripped her heart.

She'd like to be a mom someday. If only the right guy would come along. Once upon a time, after a few years of flirting and close friendship, she'd thought maybe she and Derek would eventually get together, but he'd run away to France before declaring any sort of feelings for her. As far as Ashley knew, her love was every bit as unrequited as that of Julia Roberts's character in *My Best Friend's Wedding*.

A sigh escaped her lips, but not without Jules's notice.

Her aunt raised an eyebrow. "Wanna talk about it?"

"Not really." Well, she did. With Shannon. Aunt Jules had always been so strong and independent. Ashley wouldn't want her aunt to think less of her for the way she had absolutely crumbled inside yesterday when she'd seen Derek again for the first time in over a year. But maybe her aunt could provide the swift kick in the pants she needed. "I—"

"Derek!" Ashley's mom called from the foyer. "Come on in, come on in."

Ashley sank down in her seat when Mom entered the room, Derek shuffling behind her, Claire's hand in his.

Aunt Jules glanced from Derek to Ashley, her eyes full of sympathy.

Great. Just what Ashley needed.

She squeezed Ashley's shoulder. "Sorry, kiddo."

"It's fine." Why was he here?

But that was answered in two seconds flat when her brother, Ben, came jogging around the corner and pulled Derek into a hug. "Dude, you made it."

"Thanks for the invite." Funny how two guys who'd been best friends their whole lives could go without speaking for a year and be totally okay with picking back up where they'd left off.

And yet, yesterday Derek had acted like Ashley was the last person in the world he'd wanted to see. Why? What had she done to deserve that kind of treatment? *He* was the one who hadn't returned her calls.

Derek sneaked an arm around Claire's shoulders. "It's been a while since I've had a home-cooked Baker meal." His eyes scanned the room, and Ashley tensed, wishing she could make herself as small as possible. She shouldn't have worried though. His gaze passed right over her, moving back to Ben after he'd smiled politely at a few of the Baker relatives.

The noise in the room increased once more, so Ashley was

spared having to listen to Derek introducing Claire to Ben. They laughed like they'd all been best pals forever.

"Sure you don't want to talk about it?"

"I'm sure." Ashley's teeth ground together.

"Don't let a man take away your light, Sunshine." Her aunt lowered her voice. "Use that anger to make him sorry."

Ashley jerked her head back to stare up at Aunt Jules. "I'm not angry."

"Maybe you should be."

Before she could fully consider her aunt's words, someone whistled near the front of the room.

"Hey, everyone. Could I get your attention for a minute?"

Ashley looked up to find Ben and his girlfriend, Bella Moody, standing there, Derek and Claire having moved on to chat with Ashley's dad.

Ignoring them, Ashley waved at Bella, but her friend didn't seem to see her. Not surprising since she only had eyes for Ashley's brother at the moment. The two had been nearly inseparable since they'd met last summer at Ben's inn. She'd subsequently become the manager of the place. Ben liked to tease her about how she'd shaken his world, and she'd reply that that had actually been the earthquake that originally brought her to Walker Beach.

Yeah, they'd turned each other into total cheeseballs, but Ashley loved it, especially since Ben had been devastated by love before Bella came into his life.

Maybe that meant there was hope for the rest of them with broken hearts.

Despite the urge that struck with that thought, Ashley refused to look at Derek.

The group quieted down, and those who'd been in the kitchen slipped into the edges of the living room. Mom caught Ashley's eye and grinned.

Ben snatched Bella's hand. Though she wasn't all that short, next to Ashley's broad-shouldered brother, the former big-city business executive looked downright petite. "We just wanted to tell you all the good news. I asked Bella to marry me—"

"And I said yes!"

The whole family broke out into applause and exclamations. Ashley shouldn't have been surprised, and yet a giddy flutter overtook her insides. Leaping to her feet, she rushed across the room and waited for her turn to hug the happy couple. When she finally got close enough, she punched Ben in the arm and then leaned in for a hug. "It's about time, you big lug."

Ben chuckled and squeezed her shoulders. "Thanks, sis."

She turned to Bella. "I hope you know what you're doing. This guy may seem like a charmer, but he has his super annoying moments too."

"Oh, I've seen some of those already. I'll take my chances." Bella wiggled her fingers at Ben, who watched her even as others surrounded him.

Derek slapped Ben's back. "Congrats, man."

Ashley pivoted away, slinging her arm through Bella's. "I must admit, I'm glad to finally get a sister." Shannon had always been like one, but she had a sister of her own, so it wasn't exactly the same—even though the cousins were closer than the sisters. Being an only child, Bella could understand Ashley's sentiment better than most.

"Me too." Bella tugged at her brown hair streaked with blonde. "It's not every day you get a sister you also call a friend —which is why I'd love for you to be a bridesmaid."

Ashley let loose a squeal and hugged Bella.

Her future sister laughed as they pulled back. "Guess that's a yes?"

"Of course it's a yes!"

"Good. I hope you will have just as much enthusiasm for my next question."

Sounded ominous—or much more tentative at least. "What?"

"I know things are crazy for you right now, but we were wondering if you'd help us plan the wedding."

Why in the world would Bella have hesitated to ask Ashley *that*? "Nothing would make me happier." She could already imagine Bella in a gorgeous dropped-waist silk-satin gown that skimmed her hips and flared mid thigh. That style would show off her curves perfectly. "Do you guys have a date in mind?"

"Actually, we were thinking July."

The noise in the room seemed to reach epic proportions. "Of this year?"

"I know it's short notice, but your whole family will already be here for the reunion. We thought we could hold it that weekend."

"That makes sense." Oh man, what could Ashley say? Her own schedule was already booked to the max. But this was her brother, her soon-to-be sister. She couldn't possibly say no. "It might be hard to find an available venue so last minute, though."

"We thought the inn would work nicely. There's the ballroom we've been working on, of course, but I've always wanted a ceremony on the beach. And if the weather is nice, the courtyard and back patio would be perfect if we move the furniture off and add a dance floor, tables, and chairs. Plus the entire inn will be filled with family here for the reunion, so we don't need to worry about disturbing guests. And, of course, there's the nice plus that we would save money on a venue."

Hmmm. "I suppose if you're limiting the guest list to about one-fifty, maybe one-seventy-five, the courtyard would fit everyone. But the Bakers alone would take up the majority of those spots." They had nearly one hundred coming to the reunion as of her last count.

"That's not a problem. My family isn't huge—the ones that talk to me, anyway—and most of my friends are part of your family." Bella tilted her head, something vulnerable in her normally confident eyes. She placed her hand on Ashley's arm.

"I promise I won't be one of those bridezillas. My expectations are very low. I want something simple. Just family and friends, gathered together, to watch me marry the man I love. And I can't think of anyone better to help us make that happen than you."

Tears pricked Ashley's eyes. She leaned her head against Bella's. Though she couldn't think of any free spots in her schedule offhand, she'd just have to create some. "Of course I'll help. We may have to call in some reinforcements, but there's nothing I'd like more than to help you have a beautiful day."

"Really?"

"Yes, really."

"You're the best." Bella shot Ben a thumbs-up, and he grinned and mouthed "Thank you" to Ashley.

Warmth traveled up her spine. She mouthed back, "You're welcome."

Ashley didn't know how she was going to manage it all, but she'd do anything for those who needed her—especially those she loved.

Even if the effort killed her in the process.

CHAPTER 3

*W*hy would anyone want pearls on a wedding cake?

Derek tried to maintain a neutral face at Claire's declaration. "That sounds … nice."

His fiancée pouted her lips. "I can tell you are not pleased by that idea." She turned to Ashley. "What do you think?"

"It doesn't matter what I think." Ashley sat across from them at a small table situated toward the back of Whimsical Weddings' showroom. She scrunched her nose as she absently tapped the end of her pen against the clipboard in front of her.

"*Oui*, I want to know your opinion."

"It looks really elegant if done right. You just don't want to overdo them."

"Of course not." Claire opened her binder—how she'd pulled all of that together in the five days since they'd arrived in town was a mystery to Derek—and flipped to a page featuring a picture of a tall, white monstrosity slathered in froufrou beading and frills. She slid the binder toward Ashley and pointed. "This is what I had in mind."

"I'm sure the local bakery that handles all of our custom cake orders will be able to do that, no problem."

"Wonderful."

They moved on to basic decor, and Derek tuned out the conversation. If it were up to him, they'd get married on the beach with their immediate family and have a barbecue afterward. But that would never suit a sophisticated woman like Claire. And if she wasn't going to marry for love, she could at least have the wedding she'd always dreamed of before that jerk of an ex-fiancé had pulverized her heart.

Derek checked his watch. He should be back at the vineyard, helping his dad, assessing the things that needed to change once his company partnered with Claire's. They'd have to wait until her grandfather officially turned over the reins of the company to her, and there was no telling how long that would take. Campbell Wines just had to stay afloat till then.

"Derek? Are you listening?" Claire's voice broke through his thoughts.

He glanced up at both of the women, but his gaze was drawn to Ashley. Much as he tried, he couldn't help the searing in his gut at the sight of her effortless beauty. Today her hair was tucked up in a sort of high bun, and long earrings dangled from her lobes, showing off the curve of her long neck.

Clearing his throat, Derek moved his eyes to Claire, who studied him with reserve. "Sorry. What did you say?"

Claire had the good grace to laugh, turning toward Ashley, who'd plastered a tight smile on her face. "This man is constantly thinking about work. Have you ever met such a ... how do you say it?"

"Workaholic?"

"*Oui*, that's it. Workaholic." Claire nudged Derek. "But surely you know this about him since you are friends."

He hadn't come completely clean with Claire about Ashley and just what she'd meant to him. Derek grimaced. She deserved his full honesty, but he had no desire to plunge into the past. Besides, it didn't matter. It was ancient history.

"Derek has always been really good at his job. Passionate." Ashley's fingers clenched around her pen. "But I don't know if I'd call him a workaholic. Or at least, not the Derek I knew." Her words had an edge to them.

"I guess people change, right?" Derek covered Claire's hand that rested on the table. She looked up at him, eyebrows knit together. "But speaking of work, I should probably be getting back. Are we almost done here?"

Ashley snorted, and her hand flew to her mouth. "Sorry. It's just …" She looked at Claire. "Do you want to tell him or should I?"

Claire moved her thumb along the edge of Derek's, mirth in her expression. "I am sorry, Derek, but we have hours of planning left. Weddings don't just materialize out of thin air."

"They should." He'd muttered the words under his breath but straightened when he saw he had Ashley's attention. Claire, thankfully, was busy looking through her binder again.

Ashley fiddled with an earring. "It's not unusual for a bride and groom to have different views of what they each want in a wedding, but it helps to talk through those. I have a questionnaire here that might be useful."

"Whatever Claire wants is fine."

"Don't be ridiculous, *mon cher*. This is your wedding too."

He knew Claire meant it, but come on. He'd wear a clown costume and eat oysters for their wedding feast if she wanted him to—anything to secure the future of Campbell Wines.

He squeezed her hand. "Really."

But Claire could be just as stubborn as he was. She looked back at Ashley. "I'd like to go through the questionnaire, please. That way, we can both make sure we are getting out of this what we want."

He drew in a sharp breath at her phrasing. At times, he

almost felt guilty for using Claire. But then he remembered this was what she wanted too. And they'd be happy together. Comfortable. She was gorgeous and business savvy and kind. What else could he really want in a life partner?

"Okay, then." Flipping to a new page on her clipboard, Ashley studied it. A grimace passed over her face, but she quickly recovered. "What is the moment you knew you loved your fiancé?"

"That one is quite deep to begin, isn't it?" Claire's voice remained strong.

"Yes, sorry," Ashley said. "Guess it gets right to the heart of the matter. Literally speaking."

Derek watched his fiancée, curious how she'd answer. It's not like they were exactly telling people they weren't really in love. But Claire wasn't a liar either.

Claire met his gaze. "I was engaged to someone else for three years, and when things didn't work out with him, I thought I'd never find someone else to share my life with."

She was being way too generous in her tale. After the way the guy had left Claire on the eve of their wedding because he'd received his "dream job" in New York, her ex was lucky Derek didn't know him or he'd be sporting a permanently broken nose.

"That's terrible. I'm sorry." And Ashley really looked it. How did she do that—care so deeply about everyone, even those she barely knew? It had always amazed him.

But he wasn't thinking about Ashley right now. He wouldn't. Couldn't.

Claire continued. "It was a difficult season, but when I met Derek, I knew there was something different about him. He was steady, true. Someone I could count on. And that's when I knew he was someone I could marry."

Ah, he'd seen what she'd done there—avoided the idea of love altogether.

Ashley seemed to swallow hard. "And you, Derek? When did you know …" Her voice wavered.

Why did *she* seem uncomfortable? That didn't make any sense at all. Neither did the tension—almost angry in nature—that had rolled off of her in waves last Sunday at the Baker family dinner. If anyone should be out of sorts, it'd be him. He was the one who had loved her, after all. The one who had asked her on a date. The one who had been stood up for said date.

But he was fine. Cool as a cucumber and all that. Love was just an illusion, temporary, fleeting. He had much bigger things to worry about.

Derek considered how to phrase what he felt for Claire, but at that moment, her phone rang. She glanced at it and frowned.

"What's wrong?" He snuck a peek at the phone, where Claire's aunt's face flashed on the screen.

"I don't know." She answered the call. "*Salut, Tante. Quoi de neuf?*" Then she stood and headed for the front of the showroom.

He'd picked up a lot of French while living overseas, but when two French people got to speaking, it was usually way too fast for him to interpret. Being as he was only hearing half of the conversation, it was nearly impossible.

"I hope everything's okay." Ashley's voice revealed her genuine concern. She played with her pen, clicking the end in and out in rapid succession. Her and that adorable nervous habit.

Without thinking, he reached across the table and stilled her hand.

Her eyes shot to his, igniting a connection he'd thought broken a long time ago—the one he'd read way too much into once before. He wouldn't make that mistake again.

Derek removed his hand and settled it back onto his side of the table. The silence between them swayed and bulged until it reached epic proportions.

As Claire's voice rose and fell, she paced the front of the room. He should go check on her, but something kept him rooted to his seat.

Claire hung up the phone and walked back, one hand on her forehead. "I have some troubling news."

"What's wrong?" He stood.

"Grand-père has fallen and broken his hip." Though she didn't shed a tear, her chin trembled a bit. She'd already watched the beginnings of dementia take hold in him the last few years, so this had to be a rough blow to think of him in physical pain too. "He will be all right, but needs me to come home right away to help run the vineyard during his recovery."

"Of course you should go." He pulled her into a hug. "I'm glad he's okay."

A deep breath shuddered through her. "Me too. Thankfully, his break is not terrible. My aunt said that despite being in his seventies, he is in good health and there's a chance recovery from surgery could be as little as four to six weeks." Claire pulled back to look up at him. "Of course I will be sad if he can't be here for the wedding, but I want to proceed with our plans."

"If you think that's best." Though how she was going to plan a long-distance wedding while working full time, he had no clue. But if anyone could do it, Claire Boivin could.

"I do." Stepping out of his arms, she pivoted toward the table, grabbed the binder, and pressed it into Derek's grasp. "And I will need you to work with Ashley in my stead."

Across the table, Ashley visibly stiffened.

The binder might as well have been a twenty-pound weight in his hands. "Come again?"

Claire patted his arm. "You can do this. All the details are here, but if there's anything you want to change, I give you permission to do so. And Ashley will help with those things I have not yet thought of."

"What? No. This isn't … I need to help my dad with the vineyard while I'm here." And there was no way he could be around Ashley that much. Claire provided a nice buffer, but without her, he couldn't even imagine the awkwardness.

She tugged him away from Ashley's listening ears. "Derek," Claire said in a low voice. "I know that is important, but if you want to marry me and join our companies, help our families right now, we need to plan a spectacular wedding. No expenses spared. Otherwise, Grand-père will suspect the reasons we are marrying so soon and might deny my help."

In other words, he'd refuse to give up the reins of his company, even to his own detriment. Claire had confided in Derek about how the long hours, the pressure of caring for the vineyard that had been in their family for centuries, had worsened Marcel Boivin's mental state. And while some might suspect Claire's motives, Derek knew her only true desire was to take the weight from her grandfather's shoulders, to give him the stress-free retirement he deserved.

If only Marcel wasn't so old-fashioned as to think Claire needed a man to help her "handle the business." But his stipulations had always been clear, and even with his encroaching dementia—which he was far too proud to admit to—he'd never consent to their marriage if he thought Claire planned to divorce after a year or two.

That wasn't their plan, of course. Much as he might not believe in lasting love, Derek had every intention of honoring his marriage vows.

He scrubbed a hand across his face. "You can count on me."

Claire placed a hand on his cheek and smiled. "And that is why I'm prepared to tie my life to yours. You are the most trustworthy man I know. I am confident you will not fail us."

Derek's chest may not swell with love at Claire's words, but they filled him with some sort of peace all the same.

Until his eyes swung toward Ashley, who wrote something on her clipboard. The light from the sun setting outside the window framed her, making her hair glow like some ethereal being.

He forced down the acid clawing at his throat and gripped the binder until his fingers hurt. Leaning over, he kissed Claire on the temple. "Do you need me to drive you to the airport?"

"*Non.* You are needed here. I will ask one of your sisters or call a taxi. But is it all right if I drive the car back to the vineyard? You can find a ride back?"

"Yeah, of course."

"*Merci.*" She stepped toward Ashley and cleared her throat.

Ash looked up from her notes. "Everything okay?"

"Unfortunately, I need to leave town for a while. I'm not sure when I will return. Derek will handle the planning while I am gone. I trust this will not be a problem?"

"N-no. Of course not." Ashley sounded about as sure as Derek.

"Wonderful. Please do not hesitate to call me if you do need something." Claire tapped her nails together. "I have purchased a wedding dress at the boutique in town, and they've assured me it will be ready for alterations in three to four weeks. Other than that, I will trust you both to do wonders in the short time."

"Of course." Ashley stood and held out her hand, which Claire shook. "Derek and I will make sure you both have the best wedding in the world."

Yes, they would. Working with the woman he used to love to plan a wedding with the woman he pretended to love was a small price to pay for a secure future for his entire family.

It would be simple. Derek just had to keep his eyes on the prize.

And off of Ashley Baker.

∿

This was a disaster.

Thirty minutes into planning Derek's wedding without Claire there to assist, and his one-word answers were about to drive Ashley batty.

She ran her tongue over her teeth and exhaled slowly as she studied her checklist. "Do you have the guest list finalized yet? We really need to send the invites out ASAP."

At Derek's blank look, she sighed. "Remember when we met last week? You guys picked out the invitations you wanted, and the printer did a rush order. But I need to forward the guest list so we can get them addressed."

"I'm not sure if it's finalized yet." Derek checked his watch for the millionth time and shifted in his seat.

Did the man really want to be out of her presence so badly? Why?

One thing was certain. Their friendship had clearly meant more to her than it had to him.

"Use that anger to make him sorry." Aunt Jules's words from last weekend ran through her mind. Ashley had every right to be angry, and in some ways, she was. But mostly, there was a yawning emptiness where their friendship had once taken up space in her heart—and oh, if she could only fill it again.

A sound stirred from Kyle's office in the back. He'd yet to emerge from his own client meeting. When he did, she didn't want him to see how stressed this whole thing was making her. She just needed to stay focused on what she wanted—and that was a phenomenal event that would prove to him she should get the business.

All she had to do was forget who the event was for and everything would be hunky-dory.

Ashley reached for the binder sitting open in front of Derek. "May I?"

Without a word, he slid it across the table. "Be my guest. I have no idea what that thing holds or how it's organized."

"I gathered as much." Shooting him a wry grin, she started to flip through the hundreds of sheet-protected magazine pages and printed lists. Finally, her eyes stopped on what she needed. "Here's the list. Can you text or call Claire and make sure it's the final one? And get her to send it digitally?"

"Sure." He didn't move to write it down.

Oh brother. Ashley picked up her phone and shot off a text reminder.

Derek's phone buzzed on the table and he glanced down at it, quirking a brow when he saw her message. "Thanks."

"Nice to know your phone works after all." Ooo, she should not have said that. Before she could gauge his reaction, Ashley hurried on. "Next, let's talk flowers."

"I'm sorry, but is there any way I can just … I don't know, leave that with you, and then you can call or text if you have specific questions?" Derek ran a hand along the back of his neck. "You'll probably get way more information from that binder than from me. I have no idea what Claire wants." He grimaced. "For the wedding, I mean."

"Didn't you guys talk about this?"

"I can't be the only groom in the world who doesn't care about the wedding details."

"No, but usually the bride has talked the groom's ear off about them enough that he has some clue." What was their story, anyway? It hadn't escaped her notice that when she'd asked Claire about love, the woman had responded with the moment she'd known she wanted to marry Derek. She hadn't said the L-word at all.

But marriage and love obviously went hand in hand. She was reading way too much into this. Of course Derek and Claire were in love.

Pressing her hand against her chest, Ashley cleared her throat. "Forget I said anything. I'll take the binder and see what I can gather from it. But there are still a lot of things I'll need you for."

"Like what? How much time is it all going to take?"

Argh, this man. When had he become so difficult? This was *his* wedding, after all. "I'll probably need you for a handful of appointments, like menu tasting with the caterer, final music selection, a walk-through of the venue, et cetera." She clicked her pen, then stopped, remembering Derek's reaction earlier—the warmth of his hand on hers, even for the briefest of moments. Ashley set the pen down. "I'll help guide you, if you'd like. But I can't make those final decisions for you. Well, I could, but I'm willing to bet Claire and I would make different decisions about nearly everything."

"Why do you say that?" And there, for a second, she saw the old Derek peeking through from behind his eyes—curious about her life, interested in what she had to say. But before she could speak, he waved a hand in the air. "Never mind. Just text me the dates when you get the appointments set up, and I'll make sure I'm available. We'll do what we have to, to make this happen."

Goodness, he made it sound like a business transaction. "I'll make it as painless as possible, I promise."

His frown said he wasn't so sure.

"All right, I think we're done for the day." She closed the binder and stood.

"Great." He followed suit and stuck his hands into the pockets of his cargo shorts. "I guess I'll see you in a few days."

"Sounds good." Picking up the binder, she turned, then paused. "Wait. Did Claire take the car?"

"Oh. Yeah."

"So you need a ride home."

"I'll call my dad or stepmom. They can come get me. Or I can walk."

"It's like five miles to your house." She glanced at the clock on the wall. "And it's already seven."

"Not a huge deal."

She rolled her eyes. "That's ridiculous. You can't walk all that way in the dark on that poorly lit two-lane road. That's not safe at all. I'll take you. We'll just have to walk to my apartment first to pick up my car."

Her stomach growled, and an idea popped into her head. No, she shouldn't suggest it. But why not? Somewhere inside this uptight guy was her friend, and if things stayed like *this* between them, she was never going to be able to focus enough to put on a fabulous wedding. Maybe she could eventually get around to asking him why he'd never returned her calls. "Want to get dinner at the Frosted Cake and eat on the beach?"

His jaw slackened, and he looked away from her for a moment.

Ashley took a step closer. "For old times' sake?" Ugh, her voice reeked of timid desperation. She should leave well enough alone, but she felt the need of it down to her toes. If she could just get him away from all this, maybe they could rediscover the friendship she'd once cherished more than almost anything in the world.

"Okay. For a bit."

She had to keep herself from throwing her arms around his neck in a triumphant hug. This was a step in the right direction. No, it couldn't be the same between them as it once was—not like it was from her perspective, anyway. But since love had been entirely one-sided, she'd just make sure to keep hers in check.

Ashley refused to embarrass herself with obvious unrequited emotions again. This time around, she'd conceal her feelings so well that no one in town would suspect them.

Then maybe she could finally move on from this pull he had on her.

After she tucked the binder and her other papers into the desk in her office, she led him out the front door and onto Main Street just as the streetlamps popped on. They maneuvered through the North Village, which was chock-full of adorable artisan storefronts like her Aunt Louise's Oil Me This, Carlotta's Clothing Boutique, and Fleur de Lee, the florist shop where Ashley liked to do all her wedding business. When Ashley was younger, a few blocks of the South Village had housed the majority of businesses in Walker Beach, but the downtown had expanded, stretching farther north in recent years.

"Wow, is that all damage from the earthquake?" Derek pointed at a few stores with boarded-up windows and crooked signs. Across the street, the old library building still sported a tarp over its roof.

"It hit the North Village particularly hard." Ashley adjusted the strap of her purse. "Some of the houses up in the hills got it pretty bad as well. And Ben's inn, though he's been able to reopen since then."

"Yeah, he mentioned that." A pause. "His fiancée seems nice." Finally, Derek's voice held something other than rigid militarism.

They crossed into the part of town designated as the South Village. There wasn't much foot traffic, but most shops had closed up for the night. A man and his daughter passed them on the sidewalk, forcing Derek to the side for just a second. As he skimmed past her, their arms brushed, sending a jolt to Ashley's spine.

"She's great. We're good friends." Ashley quickened her steps. "Did he tell you they're getting married later this summer?"

"In all the ruckus the other night, I didn't hear that. Let me guess. You're planning their wedding too?"

"How did you know?" Ashley stuck her tongue out at him, grinning when her actions elicited the smallest of smirks.

"Because Ashley Baker can't say no to save her life."

"Maybe she just doesn't want to."

"Nah, I think it's a compulsion."

41

The truth of his comment stung, though she wasn't sure why.

They arrived at the Frosted Cake, and Derek opened the door, indicating she should go in first. Murmuring her thanks, Ashley stepped into the diner, greeted by swirls of delicious down-home cooking. Once upon a time, this had been merely a bakery, but its owner had expanded the menu without bothering to change its name. The bright and cheery place was booming, not unusual even for a Wednesday night such as this, and there was a line to get seating in the dining room. Thankfully, the To Go counter didn't appear quite so busy.

Ashley moved in that direction, and when Derek appeared beside her, she couldn't help but breathe in the woodsy scent of his cologne. At least France hadn't changed the way he smelled.

Josephine Radcliffe swept toward them, her shock of white curls framing a round, smiling face. "Derek Campbell, is that you? You look a whole foot taller than the last time I saw you." On the wall behind her, starfish and netting hung on the edges of the chalkboard menu.

Derek chuckled. "I'm pretty sure I've been done growing for about ten years now, Ms. Josephine."

The café owner tapped the end of her nose. "I know what I'm talking about, so you just best believe me. What'll it be tonight?"

Once they'd put in their order, Ashley perused the pastry case while Derek hit the restroom. Behind her, the café door opened and blew in a breeze.

"Ashley? Hey!"

Ashley turned to find two of her favorite people in the world. "Hey, Mad. Hey, Evan."

Madison Price stepped forward and gave Ashley a hug, then pressed back into her boyfriend's side. "Working late again? You want to join us for dinner?"

"No, I've got plans, actually."

Madison lifted an eyebrow behind the purple, large-framed glasses she sometimes wore. "With who?"

"Just a client." Her friend was so busy with the newly reopened library these days, Ashley hadn't had a chance to update her on Derek's arrival. "Besides, I wouldn't want to intrude." With Madison's new job and Evan working as Walker Beach's head community developer, overseeing the Christmas festival committee, and studying to become a physical education teacher, the two didn't get to see each other as much as they'd like.

"You sure?" Madison's nose scrunched.

"Yes. I'm fine."

Derek stepped back into the room.

Ashley peeled her eyes off of him and looked back at her friend. "And like I said, I have plans."

Madison and Evan swiveled their heads at Derek's approach, and Evan's face broke into a smile. "Derek! How are you, man?"

Meanwhile, Madison fixed Ashley with a look—one that asked all sorts of questions Ashley couldn't answer. "A client, huh?" Her whisper hissed between them.

"Shhh. I'll explain later."

Derek reached forward and shook Evan's hand. Both guys were handsome and fit, though Derek was a bit taller with broader shoulders, while Evan had a leaner build indicative of the baseball player he'd once been. "I'm good, dude. And you?"

"Busy as ever, but things are good." Evan squeezed Madison's waist. "Better than good. This is Madison, by the way."

"I feel like we've met. Weren't you friends with Ashley in high school?"

"Yeah, she was just about my only friend. I wasn't exactly Ms. Popular like her." Madison's eyes danced with mirth.

"Oh, whatever." Ashley shook her head. "You were just shy."

"Something like that." Madison poked Evan in the ribs, a look passing between them before they laughed.

Ms. Josephine called their number and Ashley stepped forward to accept the paper bag with a thank you. Rejoining the group as they chatted, she caught a mention of the beach festival taking place at the end of the year.

Evan nodded to Ashley. "I'll see you at the meeting on Saturday, right?"

"Of course. I wouldn't miss it."

A moment of silence hung among them, and Ashley held up the bag of food. "Our order's ready."

Derek shook himself. "Oh, great." He turned back to Evan and Madison. "Nice to see you both again."

"Likewise, man," Evan said. "We should hang out sometime. I know Ben's looking for help remodeling some rooms in the inn so they're ready for the summer season."

"I'd love to help if it fits in my schedule. Just text me." He nodded to Ashley. "Ready?"

Her blood flashed hot at the word—and the way he said it low, as if only meant for her ears. "Yep."

They said their goodbyes and headed out the door and toward the beach. Not too far away, a couple sat in front of a bonfire, which provided enough light for Ashley and Derek to choose a spot on the pristine sand to settle into. Tonight, the moon and stars were partially obscured by clouds, and a breeze blew up from the ocean.

Ashley shivered. She should have brought a sweater.

"Here." Derek shrugged out of his blue long-sleeved shirt, which he'd rolled to the elbows. Underneath, he wore a plain white T-shirt.

"Oh, no. I'm fine."

He held it out to her. "Don't be stubborn. You're cold."

She frowned, but took the soft shirt from him, and as she did, their fingertips brushed. Shivering some more, she pushed her arms through the holes and settled the shirt over her shoulders. The cologne she'd smelled earlier now surrounded her, and she caught hints of melon and sage that she'd missed before. "Thanks."

"No problem." Reaching into the bag from the Frosted Cake, Derek pulled out a few clear to-go containers and handed her one. "So, you're helping with that festival Evan was talking about? The one that's supposed to help the economy recover from the earthquake?"

She cracked open her container and smiled at the turkey club and pickle spear sitting inside. There was such comfort in the familiar, and Ms. Josephine's food was one of them. "Yes, I'm kind of running the show. Evan's doing a lot too, but it's only part of his job."

Derek took a bite of his burger and chewed, staring out at the breaking waves. "And you're also working full time *and* helping Ben plan his wedding?"

"And hopefully buying the wedding business from my boss in a few months." Chomping down on her sandwich, she grimaced. Why had she told him that?

"Wow. That's big. Congrats. I know you always wanted to own a wedding business."

He remembered that? Ashley swallowed and set her sandwich down, wiping her hands with a napkin. "Thanks. And yes, it's exciting, but also a bit nerve wracking. There's just a lot riding on ..."

Yeah, she definitely shouldn't tell him *that*.

"On what?" Derek polished off the rest of his burger and leaned back on his hands, finally turning his head to look at her.

Tiny wings flapped in her gut, tickling her insides. "Oh, um, on your wedding, actually."

"How's that?"

"My boss said if I prove that I can successfully handle a last-minute, upscale event like your wedding, then he'd sell me the business. Otherwise, it might go to his niece."

Derek was quiet for a moment. The shadow of flames from

the bonfire several feet away danced across his face. "Sorry." He whispered the word, so she had to lean in to hear. "That it's so last minute."

And here was her chance to dig in, to learn more about him and Claire, what made them tick. What he loved about her. Why they worked. And why they were in such a hurry to get married.

Here, in the quiet, all she had to do was ask.

But did she really want to know? Maybe they had a very private reason for the rush—one that would become evident in less than nine months. Hadn't Claire mentioned having a fairly traditional family?

The thought made Ashley queasy.

Straightening, she tugged off the shirt he'd loaned her, folding it in half and gently setting it back in his lap. "It's my job to make your day perfect, no matter what. I just want you both to be happy."

And what about you?

But just like she always did when the voice in her head got brave enough to speak up, Ashley shoved the thought away into the distant corners of her heart where she wouldn't have time to really chew on it.

CHAPTER 4

There was nothing like being underground, away from all the stress and noise. Here, in this cool cellar cut into the side of a hill, Derek allowed peace to fill his lungs for the first time since he'd arrived back home.

He ran his fingers along the strong wood of a nearby barrel and inhaled the damp, earthy scent of his surroundings.

"You look happy, Boss." Mateo, his cellar master, came up beside him. Though a foot shorter than Derek in height, his broad shoulders and strong back more than made up for it. "Good to be home, eh?"

"It is." Good to be home ... and away from wedding planning.

Away from Ashley.

If yesterday's meeting and subsequent dinner on the beach were any indication, he'd be best off leaving the planning to her. By herself. Without him. Because somehow, despite all his reservations, she'd needled her way past his defenses—and he couldn't let that happen again.

"Boss?"

"Yes?" Derek shook himself from the memory of Ashley sitting on the sand snuggled in his shirt. Even this morning, the thing had still smelled like some sort of tropical fruit.

"I asked if there was anything I could do for you." Mateo's bushy eyebrows came together like two caterpillars crawling close.

A shout echoed from the back of the underground enclosure —probably some cellar rats hard at work.

"I wanted to chat with you about our barrels." Derek rapped his knuckles against the one to his left. "I'd like to ask Donovan about crafting us some made from Limousin."

"That's a European oak, right?"

"Yes, and it has a wider, looser grain. The vineyard where I interned used it for their chardonnay and cognac, and frankly, it was the best of both I've ever tasted."

Mateo scratched behind his ear. "I can see what kind of pricing he'd give us on those. How many would you want?"

Though the partnership with Claire's vineyard would provide extra resources, Derek needed to conserve in the meantime. "Let's see what price he comes back with and then decide."

"You got it."

"And one more—"

"Derek, there you are."

He turned to find his youngest sister, Heather, behind them. Wisps of hair fell from her brown ponytail, and she seemed a bit out of breath.

"Everything okay?"

"Dad and Nancy just got home from his doctor's appointment." She crossed her arms. "They want to talk with us."

"Right now?" If Dad was interrupting the workday, that didn't bode well for their news.

"Yeah."

Mateo gripped Derek's shoulder and squeezed. "I'll be here until six if you need to talk some more. Stay happy, okay, Boss?"

Derek forced a weak smile as he followed Heather out into the bright sunlight. Happy. Right. What was happiness, anyway?

"I just want you both to be happy."

Ashley's voice floated back to him on the breeze as he trudged with his sister through the vineyard toward the house. The fact Ashley could wish him well meant she felt nothing but friendship for him—if even that.

That was good. Because knowing the truth meant he *could* be happy with Claire.

Maybe just not as happy as he would have been with someone he loved. But then again, look at his parents. They'd loved each other once upon a time, and then his mom had left, never to be heard from again.

Yeah, happiness was not a realistic goal for his life, and he was better off for it.

"Why do you think they need to talk to us?" Derek caught up to Heather, who'd strode ahead as if ants bit at her heels.

Heather rubbed the edge of her eyes as she turned to him. She looked tired, but being a single working mom of a four-year-old was bound to be exhausting. "Not sure. But their moods didn't seem to indicate good news."

He picked up the pace as well, and soon they arrived at the house and headed inside. While Claire's family home was a veritable castle, the Campbells' residence smacked more of a homey vibe, with a faux bearskin rug covering the wood floor and a comfortable but worn microfiber couch and loveseat draped in homemade quilts set in a room that overlooked the vineyard.

His dad and stepmom sat on the loveseat, holding hands, and his middle sister, Christina, perched on the edge of the blue La-Z-Boy recliner. Christina stared into the empty stone fireplace, tugging on a strand of her long auburn hair as she worried her lip.

Dad bounced Heather's daughter, Mia, on his knee, wincing in the process. As soon as Mia saw her mom and Derek enter, she hopped up and ran toward them, throwing her arms around Derek's leg. "Uncle Elephant!"

"Hey, Peanut." Before she could respond, he lifted her up and tickled her belly. Her hysterical squeals filled the room, easing some of the tension from everyone's shoulders. Too bad her giggles couldn't cure the room of it altogether.

He placed Mia back on the ground, and Heather swooped in. "Millie made some cookies, baby. Why don't you go ask her for some?" Millie Rosche, their housekeeper and cook, had been with them since Derek was a child, and she helped watch Mia while Heather worked from the office attached to the tasting room.

Mia scampered out of the room, yelling "Cookies!" at the top of her lungs.

Dad gave a warm chuckle. "That girl brings so much joy into this house."

"She's the light of my life, that's for sure." Heather sat on the couch, and Derek joined her. "Now, what's going on, Dad?"

Nancy shifted in her seat.

Dad patted her hand. "As you all know, I had my six-month checkup." He paused, pulling his lips into a straight line. "It looks like my prognosis has worsened."

"Worsened? Ten years wasn't bad enough?" Reaching for a couch pillow, Heather clutched it to her chest.

"I've moved into end-stage renal disease."

Derek breathed hard through his nose. "Remind us what that means in layman's terms."

"They've given me about five years if I go on dialysis."

Five years? That … No. "Why did this happen?"

Dad looked at each of his three children for a long, meaningful moment. "We knew it would come to this if I didn't receive a transplant. True, it came sooner than we'd have liked, but I'm not dead yet."

Christina straightened. "Daddy!"

"Well, I'm not, and I'll not have you all treating me like an invalid." His voice was full of emotion. "I feel grateful God has given me as much time as he has, and we're just going to make the most of every minute we have. Okay?"

Standing up, Derek moved to the window, taking in the fields, the hills, the green. This was supposed to be a good year, a fruitful one, the year when life turned around for his family. "There's got to be more that the doctors can do."

"Not at the moment."

"That's not true."

Derek whirled as Nancy finally piped up.

She worried her lip. "Five years is just an estimate. It could be longer if he cuts back on the amount of stress in his life."

"Nancy, we talked about this."

"No, *you* talked about this, Jack."

Heather turned wide eyes toward Derek. Her response was warranted though—he couldn't remember the last time he'd heard his stepmother raise her voice.

"You've been working yourself ragged these last few months. All the stress of keeping the vineyard running hasn't been good for your blood pressure or your heart. You have to stop." Her eyes pleaded with him.

As if no one else in the room existed, Dad lifted his swollen hand to Nancy's face and lightly brushed a piece of gray hair behind her ear. "I can't let our family legacy die, Nan. I've worked too hard. My family has worked too hard. And I need to have something to leave the kids."

"Dad, we have a say in this too." Derek moved back to the couch, plopping down so hard the legs scooted back an inch. "I, for one, agree with Nancy. You have to take it easy. I'm back now and I'll take over for you." He'd just have to live here for the time being, even after the wedding. Maybe he could fly out to

France every month or so, split his life between the two vineyards. Claire would understand.

At least, he hoped so.

His father looked at him. "Much as I appreciate it, son, you have a wedding to plan. You don't have time to take over fully."

"Ashley has a lot of it covered. I can still help relieve a significant amount of the pressure."

Frowning, his dad finally nodded. "All right."

"And what about us? We can help too, you know." Heather gestured between herself and Christina. "We love our home just as much as Derek does."

"And you." Christina's voice broke. "We love *you*, Daddy."

Dad leaned forward and took Christina's hand. "And I love all of you. But while Derek actually enjoys this work, I know if it were up to you girls, you wouldn't be here anymore. You've got other dreams and goals than to be tied to this place—and to a dying father. And I will not be a burden to my children in the time I have left."

"You're not!" Heather looked nearly in tears as she huffed out the words. "We *do* want to be here. There's nowhere else I'd rather raise my daughter than right here, with her Papa and Yaya."

"All right, all right." How was his dad's tone so full of peace? He was the only calm one in the room. Ironic, since he was also the sick one.

Derek, on the other hand, was ready to rip the curtains from the window.

He inhaled a deep breath. He wasn't helpless. No, he couldn't reverse his dad's diagnosis or procure him a kidney, but he could do something to help. The partnership with Claire's company would ease their burdens financially. Once started, they'd have the funds available to hire another manager —maybe they could even get Jorge back—and then Dad could rest.

Which meant from now until Memorial Day weekend, making sure his wedding went off without a hitch would be his top priority.

CHAPTER 5

*T*oday, at least, her job would be fun.

Ashley, Bella, and Shannon huddled in a semi-circle of white rocking chairs on the raised back patio of the Iridescent Inn, Ben's B&B. Bella's maid of honor and best friend, Jessica, had experienced a last-minute car malfunction and hadn't been able to make the meeting to talk wedding plans with Bella's two other bridesmaids.

Ashley took a sip of lemonade as a breeze wafted off the ocean, rustling the papers in her notebook. "So I know you mentioned getting married during the family reunion, but have you chosen a date for sure?"

From this vantage point, Ashley could spy numerous surfers taking advantage of the Saturday morning waves. April had given way to May, and Ashley basked in the gorgeous high of sixty-eight degrees predicted for today.

Bella pulled her legs up onto her chair and hugged her knees. "We went back and forth, because we would like to spend time with everyone before leaving on our honeymoon, but we also didn't want to be overly stressed trying to get stuff done while everyone was here." She picked at some lint on her linen pants. "But I think our desire to see family outweighs anything else, so we're thinking July third."

"That makes sense." Shannon pulled her long blonde waves up into a messy bun on the top of her head. "No one will have to change their travel plans to come earlier, and those who can only come for the long holiday weekend will be able to attend the wedding."

"Exactly."

Opening her planner, Ashley examined the week of the family reunion, which was scheduled for June twenty-seventh through the fourth of July. While she agreed with Bella's logic, it would make it more difficult to focus on the family reunion events if she were doing last-minute stuff for the wedding too.

Oh well. She'd just have to figure it out and coordinate everything really well beforehand.

Ashley crossed out the family brunch and beach volleyball tournament she'd had planned for the third and penned in the wedding. Then she stood and walked to the thick wooden railing, studying the area below. Surrounded by towering trees and a plethora of bright flowers that Bella had helped Ben to plant, the courtyard gave way gradually to grass that turned to beach. Just off to the left, a bank of sandy bluffs overlooked the ocean. This piece of real estate just a mile north of town had been in her family for more than a hundred years, and Ben had taken good care of their grandparents' legacy, improving on it with Bella's help. "So you want to do the ceremony on the beach?"

"Yes, if you think that will work."

With her pen, she pointed straight out to the beach. "Are you thinking some white chairs and an arch out there, or did you want to go more elaborate?"

"Simple will be fine."

Shannon clapped her hands and sighed. "That'll be gorgeous."

"And what do you think of the courtyard for the reception?" Bella asked.

Ashley tapped her chin. "It should be fine." Yes, strung with lights, eighteen to twenty round tables with elegant tablecloths, maybe some sort of hurricane vase or floral centerpieces—she could picture it. "Better than fine. We can put the dance floor in the middle of the courtyard, tuck the DJ away near the fountain. The servers will have easy access to the kitchen. It'll be perfect."

"Yay! I'm so excited to see what you ladies come up with. Shan, I'm counting on you to make it beautiful."

Ever the efficient manager and delegator, Bella had put Shannon in charge of décor. Shannon's job as a preschool teacher gave her somewhat of an artistic outlet, but decorating for a wedding definitely had to beat gluing colorful macaroni to plates.

Shannon saluted. "Anything for my future cousin-in-law and roommate."

"Oh yeah, speaking of roommates, where are you and Ben going to live?" Ashley scrunched her nose. None of the inn's rooms were especially spacious or super private.

"Ben suggested we save money and live at the inn. I put that thought out of his head really quickly." Bella shook her head. "I had to remind the man that he's not going to be a bachelor anymore and doesn't need to live like it. So we've been looking at houses in town. Your cousin Nate has a second house in the older section of town south of Main Street. His current renters are moving out at the end of the month, so that's probably what we'll do."

Of all her Griffin cousins, Dr. Nate was probably the most well-off—though her hotshot lawyer cousin Chloe might be a close second. "Oh, that house is really cute. Three bedrooms, a big yard. Perfect for kids if you guys decide to have them." She wiggled her eyebrows then checked her watch. "Oops, sorry, don't have a ton of time. Let's talk invitations."

Bella steepled her fingers. "I know this is dumb, but that's the one thing I want that's not so simple, and I don't even know if it's possible. What do you think of wood invitations?"

"Like, invitations carved into wood?" At Bella's nod, Ashley continued. "I think they're fun and unique. But they'll be spendy."

"It's worth it to me. My mom told me that my grandparents had them for their wedding. It was their one splurge. I figured it's a way to incorporate them into my special day since they can't be there." The fact Camille had shared that much about Bella's deceased grandparents demonstrated how far she and Bella had come in mending their fragile relationship.

"You got it. I know a vendor just outside LA that does a great job with invites like that. It might take a bit longer than usual to have them made, but we should be able to get them five or six weeks before the wedding. I'll push for that, obviously."

They discussed some more details of the day, and Ashley's mind whirled. There was so much to do, and it was crucial to get as much settled in the first few weeks as possible. If they waited too long, the vendors and everything else would be too booked up. There was already a danger in that, though she had contacts she could tap if need be.

Ashley stifled a yawn. She'd stayed up way too late the last two nights trying to get as much of Derek and Claire's binder interpreted as possible, forcing herself to look through it several times before texting Derek for information. His answers had been so cold and abrupt—but what did she expect at this point?

"Ash, look at me."

She leaned against the railing and refocused on Bella and Shannon. "What? Sorry, I got lost in my own thoughts there for a minute."

"We noticed." The edges of Shannon's eyes crinkled as her lips turned down.

"I just want to reemphasize what I told you last weekend. If all of this is too much, just go as simple as possible. Because the only thing I care about is marrying your brother." Bella patted the seat next to her, and Ashley rejoined them. "Ben is the best thing that's ever happened to me. He's my family. He's home. And I ..."

Her gaze took in the ocean as Bella swiped at a tear.

Had Ashley ever seen Bella show this much emotion? The woman, who had originally come to town undercover in an attempt to buy Ben's inn, had changed a lot in the months since Ashley had met her, but she still wasn't given to crying.

Love could sure do funny things to a person, couldn't it?

It had certainly put Ashley through the wringer—still did, every time she thought about Derek.

No, no, no. She didn't love him anymore. He was different. *They* were different.

And he was in love with someone else.

Much as she wanted to read into a few little moments from their time together on Wednesday, that would be foolish.

Foolish—and dangerous.

She reached out and squeezed Bella's arm. "We are so glad you're becoming an official part of the family. I just hope you can handle all of us Bakers since we're kind of a package deal. And crazy. Right, Shan?"

Shannon laughed. "You couldn't escape us even if you wanted to. We kind of overrun the town if you hadn't noticed."

Bella let loose a chuckle. "Even if you all were horrible people, Ben would be worth it. I'm just grateful the whole lot of you is amazing."

"I'm partial, of course, but I think we're pretty great." Ashley's phone beeped at her—a calendar reminder. She checked it. "Sorry, guys. I've got to go to another client meeting." Thankfully not with Derek this time. Just a last-minute appointment to finalize details for the Dreyfusses' twenty-fifth wedding anniversary next Sunday.

"Not so fast." Shannon lifted an eyebrow. "It hasn't escaped the notice of the town gossips that you were seen in the company of Derek Campbell Wednesday night. And yet, you haven't responded to any of my texts about seeing him again. How was it? How are you?"

Her cousin had skipped the family dinner on Sunday due to a migraine. So while she knew the basics—Derek was engaged —Ashley had yet to tell her that she was the one coordinating the wedding. And somehow, the town gossips must not have relayed *that* juicy tidbit.

Ashley straightened. "I'm fine."

Bella folded her arms across her chest. "Derek. Ben's friend?" At Shannon's nod, Bella turned to Ashley. "Why is it a big deal that you were together? And why wouldn't you be fine?"

"Because ..." Shannon bit her lip.

Her cousin clearly didn't want to betray Ashley's confidence, but Ashley wasn't going to keep secrets from Bella. They were almost sisters, after all. Besides, if Ben were to be believed, Ashley's affection had once been obvious to the entire town. "Because I used to be in love with him."

She tried—hard—to emphasize *used to be.*

If only she could convince herself.

"Oh. Wow." Bella frowned. "I'm sorry."

Ashley gave a half-hearted shrug. "Like I said ... I'm fine." Oy, that attempt at nonchalance had certainly fallen flat. "I have to be. I'm his and Claire's wedding planner."

Both Bella and Shannon sucked in air.

"How can you be fine with that?" Bella's direct gaze bore into Ashley.

"I don't think she *is* fine," Shannon said, turning her attention back to Ashley. "You can't be."

"All right. It stinks. Happy? Now I've really got to go." Before she was forced to endure any more of the pity in their eyes, Ashley stood. "Bella, let's figure out another time this week to meet. Text me, okay? I'll start working on this stuff ASAP."

Protests ringing in her ears, she sprinted to her car, already regretting her sarcastic tone. Bella wouldn't care but Shannon was a sensitive soul. Somehow Ashley would have to carve out time to talk—really talk—to her cousin. Soon.

But for now, it was on to the next thing. She drove to the Whimsical Weddings office. It was dark inside—Kyle must be working from home today—and she quickly flipped on the lights, lit a freesia-scented candle, and tidied up as she waited for Mrs. Dreyfuss to arrive.

After ten minutes, she frowned. Hmm. The woman was normally extremely punctual. Maybe she'd texted. But a quick glance at Ashley's phone didn't reveal anything, so she headed to her back office and picked up Claire's binder. Might as well get some other work done while she waited.

An hour later, she'd managed to make a list of requests Claire had—some big, some small—and couldn't help but wonder what it said about her and Derek as a couple. The kind of wedding she'd have imagined for Derek was anything but fancy. He was a simple, straightforward guy who didn't care about the frills, so the fact they wanted a hanging flower installation over the dance floor and a nine-layer cake didn't jibe.

Maybe he was telling the truth, just letting the bride decide everything. But most brides and grooms had *some* details that were significant to them as a couple. So far, she'd yet to see a single one.

The bell jangled over the front door. "Ashley?"

Guess Kyle had decided to come into work after all.

"Back here!" She closed the binder and stretched her back.

Her boss appeared in her doorway, a look of concern on his face. "Are you okay? Why didn't you answer your phone?"

She moved papers around on her desk, but her phone wasn't

anywhere to be found. "I must have left it out front. I'm fine, though."

"Then why did you miss the meeting?"

"I didn't. Mrs. Dreyfuss never showed up."

"Mrs. Dreyfuss? She's coming in Monday. I meant the festival committee meeting."

Her shoulders curled forward. "What—" Oh no. That's right. Evan had even mentioned it the other night at the Frosted Cake. "I must have gotten things mixed up on my calendar."

Kyle crossed his arms and leaned his bulky frame against the doorway. "You were supposed to give out the final sub-committee assignments today. Evan did his best, but he was counting on you to show up."

It felt like a bowling ball sat in the pit of her stomach. "I feel awful." Her fingers tapped the edges of her lips. "I have the list almost complete. I'll email it out tonight."

"Ashley." Stepping into her office, Kyle dropped his arms. "I was afraid of this."

"Of what?"

"You're overworking yourself. This wedding—the assign-ment I gave you—it's too much. You're too busy."

No. She wasn't giving up that easily. "Kyle, please. I made an honest mistake. It won't happen again. You have my word." At his doubtful look, she inhaled. "Please."

"You're just lucky the festival is a volunteer thing." The man tilted his head, and his cowboy hat tipped forward. "Kiddo, take my advice. Learn to say no, or you'll forfeit the things you really want to say yes to."

"I understand."

And she did. The problem was, there was literally nothing on her current plate that she *could* say no to, not without hurting someone she loved. She'd just have to soldier on and do better in the future.

CHAPTER 6

*H*is stomach grumbled, but he wasn't hungry enough for what was coming. In fact, he might just lose his appetite altogether.

Derek called out a goodbye to his family and headed toward his car, his shoes crunching the gravel driveway. As he climbed into the Jeep, his phone rang. Slipping in the key, he waited for the Bluetooth to connect and then answered. "Hello?"

"Hi, Derek." Claire's smooth voice slid across the airwaves from the vehicle's speaker.

"Hey." It had been several days since they'd spoken. "How's your grandpa?" Derek pulled onto the road that wove through their property.

"Doing all right, considering. He grumbled so much about being in the hospital that they finally sent him home."

"So he doesn't need to stay in a rehab facility like you thought?" Dark clouds hovered in the sky, and a few fat drops of rain plopped onto his windshield as he headed into town. Nice of the weather to match his mood.

"*Non*, the surgery he had is quite advanced and won't even

require much physical therapy. A nurse will come to the house for wound care if we need it."

"That's great. How are you doing juggling the business and taking care of him?"

"Thankfully, my aunt is his primary caregiver. I'm not so inclined in that way." Claire laughed, though there was something tight in it. She had to be as exhausted as Derek had been lately. Ever since his dad's appointment eight days ago, he'd pulled fourteen-hour days at the vineyard. Not that it had fully stopped his dad from working too, but at least the strain on Dad's face had lessened a bit.

"Did the meeting with the lawyer go well?" Derek nudged the Jeep up to a stop sign and, after looking both ways, turned the SUV toward town.

"*Oui.* He came to the house today and talked through the process for passing the vineyard to me. Everything will be finalized as soon as I return from the wedding. Grand-père will finally be able to rest. Hopefully enjoy the retirement years." A clicking in the background told Derek that Claire was at her computer despite the late hour in France. "Speaking of the wedding, how are plans coming?"

"Good from what I can tell. The wedding planner has handled most of it, with just a few clarifications needed on my end." He hadn't seen Ashley in nearly a week and a half, though that was about to change. "I'm headed to the restaurant to select the courses for the reception right now."

"I have every confidence you will choose something delicious." She paused. "Will Ashley be there with you?"

"Yes." The rain turned more urgent, pelting the windshield so hard he had to put his wipers on double time. "I tried to get Heather to go with me, but Millie was out sick and no one else could watch Mia. And much as I love my niece, sitting for hours with her in a restaurant didn't sound like the best plan."

"I'm sure Ashley has done this a thousand times. She will be great."

The edges of the town emerged on the horizon. "Yeah, I'm sure." He coughed as the garbled words left his throat.

"Derek?" There was a hint of concern in Claire's normally steady voice. "Is Ashley the one?"

What in the world did she mean by that? "Of course not. You're the one, Claire." Well, in a manner of speaking. Neither of them believed in soulmates. Maybe they had at one point when they were young and foolish, but now they knew better.

"That's not what I mean. Is she the one who broke your heart?"

Several months after they'd become friends, he and Claire had told each other about their past, how they'd arrived at their current conclusions on love. But he'd never mentioned Ashley's name to Claire—at the time, even saying it had hurt. "What makes you ask that?"

"Call it female intuition."

He sighed. "Yeah, she's the one I had feelings for. But you have nothing to worry about on that front now."

"Oh, I am not worried. I know you would never do anything to hurt your family or me." Coming out of someone else's mouth, the words might have sounded manipulative, but Claire Boivin just valued honesty. She had no need to manipulate him —and yet, his gut twisted all the same. "I'm just sorry you have to work with someone who hurt you so much."

"It's no big deal. I'm over it." Main Street was rather crowded for a Friday afternoon, but after scouring the side streets, Derek finally found a place to park near the Walker Beach Bar & Grill. He cut the engine and picked up the phone. "I'm here, though, so I'd better go."

"Au revoir. We will speak soon."

He hung up, then ducked through the rain as he ran from his car to the restaurant. A mixture of smells hit his nose as he entered and scanned the room for Ashley. Huge TVs on every wall sat silent today, giving the place a much quieter and calmer feel than usual. The lunch crowd had already passed through, leaving only a handful of booths taken.

Ashley waved from a large wraparound booth in the corner, where she sat nearly at the center of the semicircle.

He walked over and slid in next to her. "Thanks for coming."

She eyed him and his blue T-shirt, which was heavily dotted with water. "I see you got caught in the storm." As for her, she didn't have a hair out of place, and the yellow shirt that perfectly complemented her tan skin was completely dry. It was one of those off-the-shoulder numbers that revealed her sculpted arms.

His mouth went dry, and he snatched the full glass of water in front of him and drank. "Yep."

Her lips twitched as she signaled to a young male server with a pocked face. "Can you let Janice know we're both here, please?"

"Absolutely, miss. Be right back."

Ashley turned to Derek. "I've taken the liberty of selecting a few appetizers, main courses, and desserts for us to try. If you don't care for any of them, we can try again next week."

He nearly laughed at how formal she sounded, but it was actually kind of cute, which sobered him right up. "I'm sure I'll like anything from this place." Plucking the plastic menu from the silver holder in the middle of the table, he nearly moaned at the pictures of street tacos, onion rings, and the restaurant's infamous grilled calamari sandwich.

"Unfortunately, that's not the kind of food we're trying today." Ashley took the menu from his fingers and put it back. "As you know, Bud and Velma Travis own this place, but their daughter Janice has started doing some catering. Her stuff is amazing, and she happened to be available on your date."

"Of course. Sorry."

"No worries." Her voice relaxed, a touch of professionalism replaced with something warm and soft. "I thought that your guests from France might want something a bit more sophisticated than ribs and burgers." Ashley pulled a straw from its wrapper.

He rubbed his throat, fingers running over a patch of hair he'd missed in his shave this morning. "Makes total sense."

"Though if I were choosing food for my own wedding, I'd pick the same food as you." She plopped the straw into her water, then stiffened, turning wide eyes toward him. "Not because it's what you would choose. That would just be my own preference regardless. More casual, you know?"

Oh man, her cheeks were growing red. She'd always flushed hard-core and rambled whenever something flustered her. Not that much did. So why was she rattled now?

He could probe—but that was dangerous territory.

Before he had to figure out what to say next, the server returned with three huge platters, which he placed on the table. Now Derek understood why Ashley had selected the largest booth in the place.

"Here we have mini gazpacho soups, tuna tartare cones, and prosciutto-wrapped persimmons. Enjoy."

"I think there was one more Janice had for us," Ashley said. "Can you double-check, please?"

"Of course."

As the server left, Derek stared at the food. He gingerly picked up one of the tuna things, which looked like peppered sugar cones—but instead of ice cream, they held some sort of tomato and green onion mixture. Ugh, and the smell ...

Ashley giggled. "It won't bite, Derek. I'm pretty sure the tuna is dead."

He looked at her, and the wry smile on her face was enough to coax out one of his own. "This is all very refined and elegant, but I can't bring myself to try them."

She picked up one of the little orange things with a sprig of greenery sticking out the top. "For someone who knows wine like the back of his hand, you sure have an underdeveloped palate when it comes to food." Taking a bite, she closed her eyes and chewed. "Mmm."

A dab of something white stuck to her lips after she'd polished off the appetizer. He stared at it for a moment before grabbing a napkin and handing it to her. "You left something behind."

"Oh. Thanks." She wiped her lips, but missed it completely.

"No, right there." He indicated the spot on his own face.

Ashley tried again, but it still clung there stubbornly.

"Here." He leaned closer and ran the pad of his thumb over the corner of her mouth.

Both of them froze at the contact, and man, he couldn't possibly miss how smooth and full her lips felt.

Dropping his hand, he swiped it across a napkin. Derek cleared his throat. "Got it."

Thank goodness the server chose that moment to return with a platter of something he did recognize. He turned toward Ashley, who bit her lip as she watched him. "Soft pretzels?"

"I know how much you like them." She fiddled with her napkin. "Or, you used to, anyway."

He sensed the hidden meaning in her words. "I still do."

"Good." A smile teased the corners of her lips. "I would have found it hard to believe your tastes had changed that much. Not after you used to order them wherever we went."

That's right, he had—at the movies, the mall, the festivals in the park.

The fair.

And then the memory struck—the two of them, not too long after he'd returned home several years after college, laughing and sharing a pretzel while the Ferris wheel spun them round and round the night sky. Before that night, she'd only ever been his best friend's little sister, but somehow, she'd gone and grown up. And she'd been radiant.

That was the night he'd known she was someone he could fall in love with.

Staring at the plate of pretzels, he held back a sigh. So they had a past. It was foolish to pretend it hadn't happened, that they hadn't been friends. Was it also foolish to think that maybe they could be friends again?

Derek picked up a pretzel, broke it in two, and handed one half to Ash. "Bon appétit."

With a full-on grin, Ashley took the offered gift and popped the bite into her mouth.

CHAPTER 7

*T*hank goodness for second chances.

Despite Ashley's appointment mix-up last weekend, today's festival meeting had gone smoothly so far. "Does anyone have any questions before we break off into our subcommittees?"

Her eyes swept the back section of the Frosted Cake, which Ms. Josephine had graciously reserved for the festival planning committee's late-afternoon meeting. In addition to the complimentary cookies the proprietor had contributed to the cause, the restaurant's expansive windows, eclectic beach-themed decor, and racks of homemade jams made it a much more inspired meeting place than City Hall.

Mayor Jim Walsh jumped up from his seat nearby and sauntered toward Ashley. "I know I speak for all of us when I say thank you for your hard work on this, Ms. Baker."

A murmur bubbled through the crowd of twenty-two volunteers. From his seat next to Madison a few tables over, Evan eyed his dad warily. Old Bud Travis, who sat on Madison's other side, winked at Ashley and gave an encouraging smile. A few of her Griffin cousins sat in the back, including Spencer, a pastor at the community church at the south end of Main Street, who flashed her a thumbs-up. His mom Elise sat next to him, pen poised above paper as she listened intently to the conversation.

Ashley acknowledged the mayor. "Of course. I'm happy to help."

"And we know how much you do for our town, believe me." Mayor Walsh placed a light hand on her shoulder. His voice rang with sincerity, but if Evan were right, his dad's only ambition was to get reelected come the fall. He hadn't even supported Evan's festival idea at the beginning. Not until he saw how the town had backed it. "If it gets to be too much, though, you just let me know. I'll be sure to get you the help you need."

His fingers—and his implication—pressed into her like one-hundred-pound weights. So much for second chances. "Will do." She turned back toward the crowd. "I'm sorry again for missing last week, everyone. Thanks go to Evan for his assistance filling in the gaps."

Evan waved it off. "No problem."

Carlotta Jenkins raised her hand, her red nails a perfect match for her bouffant hair. "I have a question." The woman's mouth was perpetually puckered as if she'd just had one too many lemons in her iced tea. "Rumor has it that you might take over Kyle's business soon. Is that true?"

Ashley bit the inside of her cheek before she lashed out at the woman she and Madison referred to as the Queen of the Walker Beach gossips. She was only asking because Kyle wasn't in attendance today. He wouldn't have taken any of her guff. "Um ..."

"I also heard that you are being forced to plan Derek Campbell's wedding to that French girl." Carlotta's mouth twisted into a sympathetic frown, but her eyes held a glint—like a shark sensing dribbles of blood in the water. "Poor thing."

Ashley's eyes snapped to the back of the room, where

Derek's sister Heather sat. Thankfully, she seemed too engrossed in a quiet conversation with her longtime friend Alex Rosche to have heard Carlotta's words.

But the whole rest of the room leaned forward with one collective breath.

Madison stood, her chair scraping against the tile. "Does anyone have a question that actually has to do with the festival? No? Fine. Get into your subcommittees, then."

The growled command got people moving, and Ashley plopped back into her chair, breathing a bit easier. She needed to make her rounds, ensuring the subcommittee chairs had what they needed to move forward until their next meeting. But for this moment, she allowed herself to be still.

Evan slid into the seat across from her. "I'm sorry about my dad. He was out of line."

"Please don't worry about it. And he was right. Sometimes it does feel like too much." Ashley rubbed the corner of her eye. Last night hadn't provided her much sleep, not after so much time spent in Derek's presence.

"Ash, we *can* get you some help, you know. You don't have to do this all on your own." Evan massaged the back of his neck.

"No, no, that's not what I meant. I just have a lot going on, but I love helping out with the festival." And who else was going to do it? She was the resident events gal, the one people looked to when they had a need to fill, especially when it came to planning and organizing. Not that others weren't capable, but everyone else was busy too, and she really liked having something of value to give to her town.

She liked being needed.

The thought unsettled her. She did it for them, not herself. Right?

Of course she did.

Shaking her head, she forced a smile. "And besides, we've made a lot of progress. The hardest part is done. Now, the details are up to the subcommittees. I'm just managing them and making sure they stay on track." That wasn't the total truth—there was still a ton for Ashley to do. But she didn't want Evan to worry. He had enough on his own plate.

"If you're sure." Evan sniffed the air and groaned. "Oh man, I can smell Josephine's meatloaf and potatoes. Having meetings here is way too distracting."

Ashley laughed. "Maybe you can convince Madison to eat dinner here tonight."

"Don't I wish. I actually need to leave soon to get an online test done tonight, and she's got new books in that need to be cataloged and shelved. It'll be a lonely night for both of us."

She could so relate. But at least they had each other. Who did Ashley have?

It didn't matter. She didn't need a man. Like Aunt Jules, she was content to be independent—and soon, a business owner. Living out her dream.

"I hope the test goes well." She stood. "I'd better talk to the chairs before they take off."

Walking around, she spoke with the heads of the sponsorship, events, and marketing and communications committees, answering questions about what she needed from them within the next month. The festival wouldn't happen until the middle of December, which was still seven months away, but those months would fly by quickly.

She steeled herself for the last conversation, but when she looked for Heather Campbell—the head of the volunteer coordination committee—Derek's sister was nowhere to be found.

Ashley's lungs released a breath.

"Here."

Turning, she found Madison behind her, holding two plates of apple pie à la mode. "What's that?"

Mad rolled her eyes and set the plates down on the table Heather and Alex had vacated. "What does it look like? Ms.

Josephine said she could tell all the way from the kitchen that you needed a pick-me-up." She slid into a chair, and Ashley joined her. "I think she must have heard the Queen's comment."

"That was terrible, wasn't it?" Ashley stabbed the pie, scraping her fork along the top of the fluffy ice cream. "Most of the time I love living in a small town. But other times ..."

"You can't let the gossips get to you. Isn't that what you told me when I first came back to town?" Madison took a bite of the pie and moaned. "Oh man, you've got to try this."

"I shouldn't. I ate like five desserts with Derek yesterday."

Madison glanced down at her own plate, poking the flaky crust of her pie. "About that. When were you going to tell me that he was engaged? I mean, I heard it from others, but why didn't I hear it from you?"

Sucking in a breath, Ashley laid a hand against her forehead. "Madison, I'm so sorry. Things have been ... but that's no excuse. I didn't mean to keep it from you, I promise."

"I've been busy too with the reopening of the library, so I understand." Madison fiddled with her fork and stared down at her pie, her lips twisting into a frown.

What was wrong with Ashley? Mad was one of her best friends. She should have made time to at least call her sometime in the two weeks since Derek had made a reappearance in her life. It was bad enough she'd been avoiding Shannon's and Bella's texts and questions about Derek since their meeting a week ago. But to have forgotten to tell Madison altogether? "I really am sorry."

"Just tell me now. What's going on?"

Forget what she'd said before. A sugar-laden pick-me-up was exactly what she needed. Ashley shoveled a bite of pie into her mouth. Then, ensuring her voice was low enough that others in the room wouldn't overhear, she updated Madison on the entire Derek situation.

"The good thing is that yesterday we finally seemed to get

past the awkwardness, which should make things easier. It felt like things were back in friendly territory, you know?" Ashley dragged the last morsel of pie along the plate, soaking it in melted ice cream before scooping it up. She hadn't tasted a single bite. Considering Ms. Josephine had baked it, that was a pure crime.

"Oh, Ash." Madison set down her fork and reached across the table, touching Ashley's arm. "It sounds to me like things between you are anything but friendly."

"I know he treated me kind of coldly at first, but really. Yesterday was better."

"That's not what I meant."

The restaurant had mostly emptied of committee volunteers, but a few early birds had headed in for dinner. Walker Beach's sheriff sat at a corner booth deep in discussion with the owner of the only bank in town. Out of the corner of her eye, Ashley spied Bill and Dottie Wildman, an adorable elderly couple who had just celebrated their fiftieth wedding anniversary. Bill pulled out a chair for his wife, who pinched his bottom and sat down before he had a chance to swat her hand away.

Ashley averted her eyes and breathed past the tightness in her chest.

"Have you thought about telling him how you feel?"

"Are you crazy?" Oops. She hadn't meant to say the words so loudly. Ashley glanced around, grateful when no one seemed to be looking their way. She lowered her voice. "He's engaged. Plus, if I mess this wedding up, I can kiss my chance of owning my own business goodbye."

"Taking over Kyle's company isn't the only way you'll ever own a business."

"But it's the best chance I have anytime soon. Starting a business from scratch takes a lot of time and money, and I don't have either of those right now."

"So figure out a way to get some things off your plate."

Madison acted like it was so easy. "Too many people depend on me. I can't let them down."

"If you're always doing stuff for other people, you won't have time for your own dreams."

"That feels selfish."

"It's not. You'll be a lot happier and a lot more capable of giving to others if your own well is full."

Madison would know. Since she'd taken over as the town's head librarian, there had been a new light in her eyes. Or maybe that had something to do with Evan.

Probably both.

Much as Ashley loved her friend, this conversation was getting them nowhere. "I'll think about it, promise." She glanced at the time on her phone. "I should go."

"So you're not going to come clean with Derek about your feelings?"

"He's engaged, Madison."

"It's not like he's married yet." Her friend's eyebrows drew together. "Ugh, you're right. I'm just so frustrated for you. I mean, you guys had a real shot at love."

"I don't know that's what I'd call a one-sided attraction."

"Why do you think it was one-sided? I thought he asked you out on a date before he left for France."

"No, I *thought* it was a date, but then I realized ... well, I was wrong."

"You sure about that?"

"Very." Ashley's brother couldn't have been clearer about her lack of a chance with his best friend.

Madison's fingers tapped the edge of her lower lip. "All I know is that the truth has a way of coming out. Remember when you urged me to tell Evan the truth about our past?"

"That was different. You were being stubborn and making assumptions about what he wanted." Ashley folded her arms and sat back in her chair.

"I could say the same about you." At Ashley's pointed glare, she held up her hands. "Fine. My point is, maybe you can't tell Derek how you feel *now*. But maybe talking about the past—how you used to feel, how things used to be—would go a long way in helping you heal. Let the truth set you free."

How could she ever tell him about the past without making her current emotions totally obvious?

Ashley stood, gathering up the plates and forks, stacking them to make it easier for the busboy. "It's a nice idea, Mad. But I'm not sure that the truth would bring anything but pain." And embarrassment. "Besides, it would only ruin the fragile bit of friendship we've managed to build."

Standing, Ashley hugged Madison goodbye and left the Frosted Cake—and Madison's suggestion—behind.

Late-night work session all by her lonesome, here she came.

CHAPTER 8

"What do you mean, we're not on the schedule?" Ashley's grip tightened on the arm of the chair where she sat across from Janessa Kennedy, the Moonstone Lodge's events coordinator. Derek shifted in the seat next to Ashley, a frown fixed on his face.

This couldn't be happening. Not with *this* wedding.

With soaring crossbeam wooden ceilings and plush furniture featuring crystal-button tufted seat backs, Janessa's office was as opulent as the rest of the luxury resort nestled in the pines just a few miles northeast of Walker Beach. Guests came from all over for the 360-degree views—the ocean on one side of the hotel and the forest on the other.

The woman's black bob swayed as she shook her head. "That's not quite what—"

"I mean, we've paid the hefty deposit." Ashley's voice gathered steam. "I've triple-checked the date with your assistant and met with him to go over details."

In fact, this was the first time she was dealing with Janessa regarding this event at all. The woman had left a voicemail on Ashley's phone this morning requesting an urgent call back.

Since Derek needed to tour the venue and make a few decisions that Ashley hadn't been able to make on her own—despite working non-stop the last three days on the wedding details—they'd decided to drop by to chat with Janessa in person.

But the coordinator's news had not been part of the plan. "How did this happen?" Again Ashley peeked at Derek, who hadn't removed his hawk-like gaze from Janessa.

How could he be so calm? He was getting married in eighteen days, and they'd just been informed that the venue wasn't available.

In all his years of planning, this had probably never happened to Kyle. And he was going to kill Ashley if Derek didn't first.

But instead of murder in his eyes, Derek merely looked like he was assessing any old business problem that needed a solution. "I'd like to know the same thing. What happened?" He sat back, folded his arms across his chest, and waited.

Ashley breathed out slowly. If he wasn't freaking out, she wouldn't either. She couldn't. Besides, anger would only serve to alienate the events coordinator of the Moonstone Lodge, one of the only wedding venues in town that was elegant and large enough to accommodate higher-end weddings. The resort's hilltop location and ocean views made it a coveted wedding locale.

Janessa had the good sense to at least look chagrined. "When Mr. Mahaney called to inquire about the date in question, my assistant didn't look at the calendar properly. While it's true that there are no outside events scheduled during the date in question, we have a very exclusive private party renting the entire lodge for two weeks, including the one before and after Memorial Day weekend."

Exclusive private party. Aka a celebrity or at least someone very rich and high profile.

"And frankly, Ashley, I'm surprised at your assumption."

Janessa's chin raised in challenge. "Everyone knows that we book up a year, sometimes two, in advance."

Janessa was right. When Ashley had found out Moonstone Lodge was available so last minute, and on a holiday weekend no less, she should have known it was too good to be true. Even though she'd talked with Janessa's assistant several times, she should have dug deeper. "I …"

"Hang on now." Derek straightened. "It doesn't sound like it's Ashley's fault at all. Sounds like it's yours."

"As I explained, my assistant—"

"And your assistant answers to you, doesn't he?"

The event coordinator's lips pressed into a firm line. "Not anymore. I let him go over this incident, of course."

"Is there anything we can do about this?" Derek asked. "Any way you can squeeze us in?"

"I wish I could, but the private party's contract explicitly states there are only to be employees on-site, and each of us has been asked to sign an NDA. So a wedding is out of the question, I'm afraid."

The air in the office crackled. "And what about *our* contract?" Though Derek's voice remained steady, it was laced with steel. "If I contact my attorney, will he tell me I have grounds to sue you for breach of contract?"

Ashley's gaze ping-ponged between them. Much as she hated that this was happening, she couldn't afford to burn bridges with Janessa.

She placed a hand on Derek's forearm. His eyes shot toward it, then up to meet her gaze.

Before she could explain her thoughts, he stood. "I don't see that there's any reason to stay here any longer. I expect a full refund on our deposit, Ms. Kennedy."

"Of course. And I can offer you a twenty-five percent discount on a future event booking." The woman smiled.

How magnanimous of her.

Ashley followed Derek out into the lobby. As soon as Janessa's office door shut behind them, she dropped her head into her hands. "I'm so sorry, Derek. I can't believe this." Tears burned her eyes. Oh no. She couldn't cry. How unprofessional.

It had gotten so quiet she was sure Derek had left her there. But after several achingly long moments, he placed a hand on her back. The warmth traveled all the way to her toes.

"Why are you sorry?" His voice had gone soft, and she looked up. "It'll be okay. We'll just get our heads on straight and start calling around, looking for another venue."

"Derek, you don't understand." Ashley stepped back, and his hand slipped away. "There won't be any more venues. It was a pure miracle this place was available."

He looked away, breathing out steadily as her words soaked in. "Come on." He put out his hand.

She just stared at him.

"Ash. Come on."

Ash. It was the first time he'd called her that since returning. And it was like a blanket thrown over her shoulders on a winter day. Like a chocolate chip cookie straight out of the oven.

Like coming home after a long trip.

Slowly, Ashley reached out and accepted his hand—and nearly sighed at the immediate warmth of her fingers tucked inside his.

Derek led her out the front door and to his beat-up blue Jeep. Without speaking, he took her notebook and purse from her, stuck them in the back, and grabbed a few water bottles before handing her one. Then Derek locked the doors and snagged her hand again.

The air was crisp and cool, a beautiful seventy degrees or so, and as they walked down the long driveway of the lodge, dead leaves and rocks crunched beneath their feet. Today, she'd opted for her nicest jeans, a blazer with three-quarter-length sleeves, and comfy flats—a good thing if she were right about Derek's intentions.

And yeah, it was most definitely wrong of her, but she allowed herself to relish the feel of her hand in his. His fingers had always been slightly roughened from all the work he did around the vineyard. But instead of chafing against her skin, his calluses served as an anchor, holding her hand more securely so it didn't slip.

They crossed the property until they got to a service road they'd frequented many times together before. A small wooden sign was the only thing marking this as a sanctioned hiking trail, one that locals had managed to keep a secret from tourists so it wouldn't become overcrowded.

As they passed the sign, Ashley's shoulders relaxed. The gentle slope of the trail, the twittering of birds high above them, the commingled smell of pine needles and ocean were all as familiar as breathing.

"Feeling a little better?"

"Yes, actually."

"Good." He dropped her hand and kicked at a rock, shoulders hunched forward as they moved down the trail.

"Thanks for bringing me here. I've always loved it." *Always loved being here with you.*

"Being out in nature has a way of calming me down." He peeked at her for a moment. "I thought it might work for you too."

"Always the problem solver."

That got a smile, albeit a sad one. "Some problems are easier than others to solve."

What other problems were weighing on his shoulders?

A slow ache ambled through her whole body. Ashley wanted her friend back—the one who had told her everything. She'd been the first person he'd confided in about the full extent of his dad's illness, what it meant, even how he felt about it.

Ashley bit the inside of her cheek. Claire was the person he'd tell those things to now. He didn't need Ashley.

And she needed to stop needing him.

"Maybe talking about the past—how you used to feel, how things used to be—would go a long way in helping you heal." Madison's words from three days ago drifted back to her.

But even if she wanted to, how was Ashley supposed to go about starting a conversation like that?

A butterfly floated past her nose and landed on a nearby log. Two squirrels scampered along the trail in front of them and raced each other up a tree. Amazingly, the only companions they'd met along the path today had been of the animal variety.

This was a world unto themselves, a sliver of time that belonged only to them. If she were going to talk to Derek —*really* talk to him—then where better to do it?

She stopped.

Derek looked back at her, tilting his head. "Everything okay?"

Ashley inhaled sharply, studying him. "Why did you only call me once when you were in France?"

A shadow crossed his face. "Ash."

"No." She marched toward him until they stood nearly toe to toe. "I need to know, Derek."

For a moment, he refused to look at her. But finally, he lowered his chocolate gaze to hers. Oh, a girl could get lost in those eyes.

But not today. Today, she needed answers. "Why, when I tried calling and texting and emailing you several times, did you act like our friendship meant nothing to you?"

He opened his mouth as if to speak, then shook his head. "It doesn't matter." Maneuvering around her, he started back down the trail toward the trailhead.

"It matters to me." She stood her ground, waiting for him to turn around. Praying he would.

His gaze remained on the path ahead. "Just drop it, Ashley."

"I can't."

"Why not?" His fingers gripped his water bottle so hard she heard the crinkle of the plastic from ten feet away. "It doesn't do any good to dig up the past."

Ugh, the infuriating man and his logic. For just once, couldn't he show he was capable of *feeling* something? "It does if it's still affecting the present or the future."

"It's not."

"Maybe for you. But it's not all about *you*, Derek!" A few birds on a nearby branch flew away as her raised voice echoed through the trees. Ashley's chest heaved.

Derek finally turned to look at her. His jaw had slackened, but he didn't say anything. Only stared.

He just didn't get it—and he never would. She'd been stupid to bring it up in the first place. What could it really accomplish except remind her that her brother had been right?

"Forget it. I'll see you later." She turned on her heel, heading deeper into the forest away from him, longing to break into a run. If she had on her Brooks, there'd be no question, but her current shoes would only leave her with a twisted ankle to go with her smarting heart.

Ashley picked up the pace, climbing the ever-increasing slope of the trail until she reached wide stone steps that led up to a treeless bluff overlooking the ocean. She'd taken the first two steps when she heard footsteps behind her.

"Ash, wait."

She pivoted. "You didn't have to follow—" But she'd miscalculated the depth of the step and twisted off the edge completely. Ashley's water bottle went flying, and her squeak got muffled in Derek's broad chest as he caught her mid-fall.

He wrapped his arms around her, cocooning her in safety. His heartbeat pounded in time with her own.

For a moment, Ashley kept her hands where they'd landed

against his stomach. Then, as if of their own accord, her fingers trailed along his middle. He sucked in a breath as she hooked her arms around his lower back and laid her head in the crook of his chest, breathing in the scent that was all his.

And she never wanted to leave, even though she knew she had to.

He rested his chin against her forehead, and they stood there, breathing, waiting—for what, she wasn't quite sure, but she didn't want anything to break the sanctity of this moment.

Finally, Derek spoke. "The reason I only called you once was because it hurt too much to talk to you."

At that, she pulled her head back to look up at him. The firm set of his mouth showed her there was no tease in his statement. No hint of a lie. Only the truth. "What do you mean?"

"You lied to me."

"What? When?"

"Before I left. We were supposed to meet at Mimosa's. You canceled at the last minute. Said you were sick."

Dread pooled in her stomach. Because yes, she had done that. She'd been so excited, thinking that Derek had finally asked her on a date. That's how she'd interpreted it, anyway. But then Ben ...

He continued. "The next day I was getting some soup to bring you and ran into Shannon at Ms. Josephine's. I asked if she knew how you were doing and she said you'd been fine when hanging out the night before."

Ashley blinked up at him. A piece of brown hair hung in his eyes, and she nearly reached up to push it away, to push away the pain in his eyes. "Derek ..."

"It's fine. Like I said, no use digging up the past. Still, I don't want you thinking of me as some jerk who didn't care about you." His gaze swept her face and he dropped his arms from around her. "But why did you lie?"

Stepping away from him, she huffed out an incredulous

laugh and wrapped her arms around her middle. "It wasn't quite a lie. I realized how ridiculous I was being, and it did make me sick to my stomach."

He lifted an eyebrow.

Great. She'd have to explain, as embarrassing as it would be. *You're the one who wanted to get things out into the open.* She could kick herself for that impulse right about now. "I'm sorry I didn't elaborate at the time. But I couldn't face you."

Ashley turned and studied a nearby tree as if the bark were the most fascinating thing she'd ever seen. Anything to avoid seeing Derek's face when he realized the truth about the depth of her feelings—what they'd been, anyway. No way was she divulging her heart's traitorous longings as of late.

She sucked in a breath of courage. "I thought you'd asked me on a date. And I was being all dumb and twirling and humming getting ready for it, and Ben stuck his head into my doorway and asked what was going on, and when I told him you'd asked me out, he shook his head and reminded me of the crush I had on you in high school—"

"You liked me in high school?"

She waved her hand, still refusing to look at him. "Yes, it was a dumb little crush when I was a freshman and you were a senior." Ben had found a notebook she'd covered in *Ashley plus Derek equals love*, and he'd laughed at her.

"Anyway, he reminded me that I'd followed you around with puppy dog eyes back then and that I was still doing it, all these years later, and that you only saw me as a friend. He didn't want me getting hurt like he had—that was not too long after Elena dumped him—and warned me that my love ... er, affection for you was way too obvious, not just to him but to everyone in town. So I canceled on you because I was afraid that you would see that I'd misinterpreted what you'd meant as just another hangout, and things would never be the same between us again."

Oh, goodness. She had *not* meant for all of that to come

tumbling out. Guess her emotions had been more stoppered than she'd realized.

Derek was quiet behind her. Served her right. She picked at a piece of bark dangling from the tree, pulling at it until it came clean off, revealing a gentle green layer.

Then he was beside her, the sides of their arms touching. "Ben may be my best friend, but he can be a real idiot sometimes."

She jerked her head up. "What do you mean?"

He stared straight ahead at the tree, at the verdant proof of life that had been hiding under the dead, rough bark. "Because, Ash. I *was* asking you out on a date. I was crazy about you."

Oh. Ooooh.

"I wonder what would have happened if he hadn't interfered." Then, finally, he looked at her.

Her heart started to pound as she studied Derek's face—the long slope of his nose, the chiseled cheekbones, the strong jaw, the piercing dark eyes. He lifted an eyebrow, but if he were waiting for a response, there wasn't much Ashley could say. The only response she wanted to give wasn't safe.

Because ... He. Was. Engaged.

"I guess we'll never know." Ashley forced herself to take a step back toward the trail. She located her fallen water bottle and picked it up. "Come on. We have a wedding venue to find."

CHAPTER 9

*N*othing allowed a man to take out his frustrations like wielding a nail gun.

Derek eyed the Iridescent Inn's wooden flooring and determined the best place for the first hole. Holding the air gun at a forty-five-degree angle, he sent a nail flying into the wood. Then he moved the gun about six inches to the left and shot again.

Yes, definitely satisfying.

"I think you're enjoying that a bit too much, man." Ben dropped the next piece of wood between Derek and Evan, who sat on his knees against the concrete with a tapping block and mallet. "Thanks to you both for coming to help."

"I don't mind one bit. Madison's hosting a book club at her house and I'm between classes, so I didn't have much going on tonight." Grabbing the new piece, Evan set it next to the wood Derek had just finished nailing. "Plus a bit of manual labor always feels nice. I haven't had the chance for much of that lately."

Personally, Derek had a ton of other things he could be

doing right now at the vineyard, but he grunted in agreement anyway and jammed another nail through the wood.

"I appreciate it nonetheless. When Bella suggested renovating these rooms, I kept putting it off. The summer season kind of snuck up on me, but we're almost done. Just the three rooms on this north part of the inn are left."

The inn had sustained heavy damage during the earthquake last year, but Derek never would have known it otherwise. Ben must have worked hours on end to get it looking as nice as it did now.

Once Evan had tapped the next wooden piece into place, Derek followed along with the gun. Ben measured the gap between the end of the wood and the wall and headed out the door to the table saw. They'd only completed two rows so far, but according to Ben, the pace would pick up once they could use the flooring nailer.

"How was France?" Evan started on the next row, pushing the grooves onto the tongue of the second row. "I can't believe you've been back for a few weeks and we're just now hanging out." He tapped the boards together.

"Sorry about that. Things have been busy." The whir of the saw in the hallway cut through the air. "But to answer your question, it was great. I learned a lot that I'll be able to implement at our vineyard. Made some great connections too. All in all, it was a good use of my time."

"I'll say." Evan grinned. "You came back with a fiancée, after all. Did you guys date for long?"

"Not exactly. We were friends first and one thing kind of led to another." Derek used his forearm to wipe away a trail of sweat from his hairline. When had the room grown so stuffy?

Glancing up from his mallet, Evan fixed him with a knowing look. "My story with Madison is kind of similar. Although she actually hated me when we first met. Well, met again for the first time since high school."

"Sounds like an interesting story." Derek didn't miss the spark in Evan's eyes when he spoke about his girlfriend. His ribs squeezed.

"It is. And like you, I don't think you have to date very long before you know someone is the one."

Derek coughed, scratching at a sudden itch on the back of his neck. "Does that mean you're planning to propose?"

"Not quite yet. She's still settling into town and her new job. But hopefully the timing will be right soon enough."

"Congrats. That's great, man. Sounds like you guys are happy."

Ben came back in with a few more pieces of wood and set them on the ground, then leaned down to mark how long the last plank in the current row needed to be. "Evan here is more than happy. He's a regular sap these days."

Evan chucked a stray piece of felt underlayment at Ben. "You're one to talk."

"Nah, just you."

"So if Bella was to walk in this room right now, you'd just keep on working then, is that right?"

"Yep."

"Liar."

Straightening, Ben rocked back on his heels. "Fine, you win. I'd march straight over to her, kiss her, and tell her I'm the luckiest man in the world for having a woman like her believing in me and challenging me to be better. That what you wanted to hear?"

"Yep." Evan started whistling as he plunked the next piece of flooring into place.

Derek listened to his friends' exchange, the ease with which they spoke about the women they loved, and something inside his chest rang hollow.

"What's this about kissing and whispering sweet nothings in my ear?"

They all turned to find Bella standing in the doorway, a clear pitcher of lemonade and a stack of red Solo cups on a tray. Behind her stood Ashley.

It was like she'd materialized straight from Derek's thoughts. His whole body flamed hot.

While Ben and Evan eagerly made their way toward the women and the lemonade, Derek got to his feet and pushed open a window. The cool breeze of early evening skimmed his cheeks, allowing him to breathe more easily. But it didn't loosen the thought that had been on a continuous loop in his brain for the last twenty-four hours since Ashley's revelation.

They'd loved each other at the same time.

They could have had something amazing.

He might not be preparing to marry Claire right now. He might be …

No. Fact was he *was* preparing to marry Claire. And doing so was going to save Dad's legacy.

Things had worked out exactly as they were supposed to.

"Derek, you want something to drink?" Ben's voice pulled him back to reality.

"Sure." He left the window open and walked over to the semicircle the other four had formed. After thanking Bella for the cup of lemonade, Derek turned to Ashley. "Surprised to see you here."

Was she following him? But that was ridiculous. Yeah, they'd both been quiet on the hike back to the lodge yesterday, but she had a lot going on in her life. Ashley Baker was going places. She definitely wasn't sitting around pining after him.

Ashley took a sip of lemonade, lifting an eyebrow as she studied him. "This is my brother's inn."

"Right." Duh. He slammed back a swallow from his own cup, coughing at the drink's sour bite.

"We were talking through a few more wedding plans." Bella

collected the guys' empty cups. "I guess we'd better get back to it."

After Ben leaned in to kiss Bella, the women retreated.

Good. Back to shooting nails.

Ben started up the saw in the hallway again.

"Speaking of wedding plans, how are yours coming, Derek?" Evan resumed his position behind the last finished row of wooden planks.

Derek sighed and plunked down beside Evan again. "They *were* going smoothly until our venue canceled on us yesterday." His hands clenched the gun's handle as he waited for Evan to be done fitting the joints together.

"No way." Evan frowned. "What are you going to do?"

"I'm not sure yet. Ashley is still calling around to see if anything else is available, but it's not looking promising."

Ben entered the room once more. "What's wrong?"

"His venue got canceled." Evan looked from Ben to Derek. "What about the vineyard?"

"You have to be licensed for events, and we're not." If they had been, the fix would have been simple. But Dad had never thought much beyond the wine. Once they had their feet under them again, though, Derek would look into what it would take to hold events there. His sisters would probably be great at managing them.

Ben pushed his safety goggles up onto his forehead. "What about having it here?"

"Here, like at the inn?"

"Sure, why not? The calendar is clear since we haven't started hosting outside events just yet, and I think a lot of our guests that weekend are your out-of-town guests anyway."

"Wow, man. That would be amazing." He didn't deserve Ben's generosity. "Let me know how much it costs, but I'm sure it won't be a problem."

"Dude, I'm insulted." Ben squatted and punched Derek on the shoulder. "No charge."

"You have to let me do something." Yeah, he and Ben had been best friends their whole lives, but Derek wouldn't mooch off of him—especially since he hadn't been the best at staying in touch since he'd been gone.

Maybe that could change, though. He'd forgotten how much he'd missed surrounding himself with good guys who could make him a better man. A stronger one.

Eyeing their progress on the floor, he put aside the nail gun and snagged the flooring gun instead. The extra power pulsed from his fingertips through his entire body.

"You're here, aren't you? Besides, we're already getting the place fixed up for our wedding, so it's not a lot of extra work."

Well, that solved one major problem on Derek's list.

Now if only he could get Ashley Baker out of his head.

CHAPTER 10

Sixteen days before his wedding, and he was just getting the first official tour of the place where he would make Claire his wife.

Of course, he'd spent time here as a kid and teen. But that was a lifetime ago.

So much had happened since then.

"This is the ballroom." Ashley stopped next to double doors leading into a large space on the upper level of the Iridescent Inn. Ben and Bella were out but had apparently given Ashley permission to do the tour solo.

If he'd known that, Derek would have brought Heather or Christina along. Or better yet, Mia. Four-year-old nieces made great buffers.

As Ashley flicked on the lights, they stepped into the room. Derek couldn't hold back a low whistle at the impressive sight before him. The huge windows faced the ocean. Being up high like this gave them a long view of the coast. And the ballroom itself was well appointed, with several chandeliers reflecting light off the bronzed, polished concrete floors. Apparently it had been a huge catchall room for years until Bella had decided to renovate it into a money-making events venue a few months ago.

"We have a few options." Ashley spun in the large, open room, and he found himself stepping closer to her for no logical reason. "We can hold the ceremony on the beach, in the courtyard, or in here, although this space is clearly better suited for a reception. It doesn't feel as intimate as I'd think a ceremony should be." She scrunched her nose as she assessed the space. "Then we could do the reception here or in the courtyard. Or any combination of those, really. What do you think Claire would want?"

His muscles tensed at her mention of his fiancée. "I'm having trouble picturing how you'd set the courtyard up."

"Let's go take a look. I'll show you my vision." She turned off the lights and led the way down the hallway. They passed a guest or two before reaching the upstairs lobby—which was really more of a large living room—then veered outside to the upper deck where several chairs allowed guests to take in the vista. A winding staircase led down to the courtyard, which was enclosed by a low stone wall and an arc of overhanging trees. Water trickled down a tiered stone fountain near the exit, a wrought iron gate that opened onto a path toward the beach. Flowers of various colors bloomed in all stages of life.

"This is really nice." He walked out onto the travertine pavers. "I can't believe Ben isn't making a fortune off of doing events at this place."

"He will. Bella's a perfectionist and wants everything to be just right before they start." Ashley followed him. "So you approve?"

"Yeah, of course. Not that I have any choice. But even if I did, I think this would be perfect."

"Good. Ben and Bella are doing their ceremony on the beach and reception here in the courtyard. What do you want?"

He considered all the options. "To be honest, I'd like to do the same, but I don't think Claire will want to worry about sand in her shoes and the wind off the ocean blowing her hair during the ceremony." The wind could be brutal at times, and it was unpredictable. But there was something strong and striking about the wild ways of nature. Still, he was making decisions for both of them, and Claire trusted him to take her desires into account. "So what are you thinking in terms of setup?"

A breeze rustled Ashley's hair across her cheeks while she studied the courtyard and walked to one end. "I think I'd do an arch here, then split rows of white chairs on either side, creating an aisle here. We can adorn the ends of the aisles with bows so everyone has to enter from the outside. And depending on how simple or done up you wanted to go, we could add some flower sprays around the arch."

He strode over. "So I'd stand about here?"

"Yes. And Claire can enter the courtyard from that lower door."

Studying the open courtyard, he tried to picture it—how it would really be to watch Claire step down the aisle toward him.

But his mind rebelled against him, imagining a smiling blonde instead of a solemn brunette heading down the path, dressed in white, holding a simple bouquet of flowers.

Get it together, man. Derek pivoted and headed toward the fountain. He leaned over to trail his fingers through the pooled water at the bottom. The cold pricked his skin, a welcome relief to the burning sensation racing through his veins.

"Derek? You okay?" Joining him at the fountain, Ashley sat on the edge. She pulled her fingers along the placid surface, and circles rippled out at her touch. Her long hair fell over her shoulder, nearly hitting the water. His fingers ached to feel the spun gold against his skin.

Listen to him, waxing poetic. He should leave. Right now. Instead, Derek lowered himself next to her. "No, I'm not. This is hard, Ash. And I'm sick of it."

Now why had he gone and said *that*? But for once, he didn't want to think. Just wanted to be near her, to feel the electricity rolling off of her, making him feel something he hadn't in a very long time.

Ashley pulled her hand back into her lap, wiping the water onto her jeans. "Sick of what?"

"Pretending."

Her delicate throat bobbed and her lips parted slightly. "Pretending what?"

The silence between them pulsed with something that begged for life. Derek scooted closer, until their thighs and upper arms touched. "That I don't feel something I shouldn't when I'm with you."

Eyes widening, Ashley studied his face in that perceptive way she had, as if she were looking deeper than the surface. And just like the water, her presence sent ripples through him, through his life, in a way he couldn't deny.

She pressed her lips together for a moment, then shook her head. "You never told me your proposal story."

The electricity between them fizzled like a bucket of water dumped on a fire. Why had she gone and brought that up?

Because she was smarter than him, that was why.

He blew out a breath and leaned forward, placing his elbows against his knees. "Uh, well, it wasn't really your typical proposal."

She waited, not saying a word.

Fine. She wanted the truth? "My sisters had told me I should come home soon. That Dad wasn't doing so hot. Claire and I were talking and just sort of decided that getting married was what we wanted. There wasn't anything really grand or special about it." In actuality, Claire had been the one to suggest the idea, but he wasn't going to go so far as to tell Ashley *that*. It still felt odd to him, since he'd been raised as a traditional sort of guy. "It wasn't how I always pictured proposing, believe me."

"How did you always picture it?"

Nearly missing her whispered words, he glanced at her. She picked at the cuticle of a fingernail so hard it had to have hurt. Before she could rip it to shreds, Derek enveloped her hand with his own.

Ashley tensed but otherwise didn't move, keeping her gaze fixed on the ground. From her petite nose to her pointed chin, the planes of her face were so familiar—so beautiful. She had these little crinkles at the corners of her eyes from smiling so much. And her lips ...

Derek wove their fingers together and ground his back teeth together before speaking again. "I always wanted to propose at the vineyard, at that spot in the very center where the vines veer from different directions and leave an open circle."

She finally looked at him.

"I thought I'd line the path from the house to the spot with those lights in bags—you know, the ones we had to sell in grade school as a fundraiser."

"Luminaries?"

"Yeah, those. Of course, I'd use fake candles inside of them. Couldn't chance actual fire in a vineyard." Derek licked his lips as he stared into her blue eyes. "And I'd somehow tie this ribbon from one end of the vineyard to that spot in the middle. Along that ribbon, I'd attach little notes, each one featuring a memory about our relationship."

Ashley's cheeks had two matching spots of red on either side. "That's so sweet."

Lowering his voice, he leaned closer. "And when she got to the circle, I'd be waiting with a ring in a little velvet box. And it would be just the two of us. Us and the stars."

Just the two of them—him and Ashley.

His brain screamed at him to stop, but his body didn't listen. With his free hand, Derek ran his thumb from her high cheekbone across her face. He traced the contour of her ear and brought his face within inches of hers, inhaling her intoxicating scent.

Ashley's eyes dropped to half-mast, and she exhaled in such a sweet way that he was a goner.

His whole body trembled as he moved in, adrenaline pumping in anticipation of this thing he had wanted for so very long. Finally, his lips hovered over hers.

"Ashley?"

Both of them jerked away at the voice echoing through the courtyard.

～

She blinked rapidly. Her brain took a long few moments to register what her eyes were seeing.

Bella.

Bella was here, and she stood with her hands on her hips, head cocked to one side, eyes narrowed.

Oh, goodness.

Ashley stumbled to her feet.

Derek stood too, steadying her, his touch scalding her arm. "You okay?"

"Yes." Her voice squeaked. She closed her eyes for a brief moment and shook her head. "No."

Bella stepped toward Ashley. "Derek, I think you should go."

Shoving his hands in his pockets, he finally looked chagrined. "Right. I'll … call you, Ash." Then he turned and walked away.

Ashley watched him go, and a tingling sensation swept up the back of her neck and across her face. A tiny moan left her lips as she buried her face in her hands. "What just happened?"

"That's what I'd really like to know too."

The trees that overlooked the courtyard had felt so intimate before, but now Ashley's throat closed at the sight of them. "I have to get out of here." She took off for the stairs, but Bella jumped in front of her.

"Not so fast, girl. You cannot just take off. You've gotta talk to me."

Ashley bit her lip and looked away. "I don't know what to say. I don't even know what to think."

"Let's walk, then. No thinking required. I just don't want you to be alone right now." Taking her hand, Bella tugged her back into the courtyard and toward the black gate. It creaked as it swung outward. As promised, her future sister-in-law didn't say another word as they made their way down the path toward the beach. Both of them plucked off their sandals and left them behind, sinking their toes into the sand.

The wind whipping off the waves stung Ashley's cheeks, but not as much as the memory of those stolen moments in the courtyard with Derek stung her heart. He'd been one second, maybe two, from kissing her.

Finally, they reached a bluff covered in a brilliant spray of wildflowers. Oranges, yellows, and reds jumped off nature's canvas, painted in broad strokes that filled her vision. They were beautiful now, but winter would come. Petals would fall, and the stalks would curl in on themselves, leaving pure memory as the only proof they'd ever existed.

Ashley squatted, ripping up the nearest grouping of flowers, then stood and flung them over the edge of the cliff into the swirling ocean below. "Why did he almost kiss me?" She curled her arms around her middle.

Her friend was beside her in an instant, snaking her arm around Ashley's side and leaning her head against Ashley's arm. "What happened?"

"One minute I was showing him the setup for his wedding ceremony, and the next he was saying things."

"Like?"

Ashley dug fingers into her sides as she studied the water.

Black rocks dotted the coast, white foam bashing against them, drowning them momentarily. "Like he's tired of pretending he doesn't feel something around me. Something he shouldn't. And I'm tired of it too, Bella."

"You still love him, don't you?"

"Ding, ding, ding." Ashley sighed. "I'm just so confused. Of course I love him. And I thought my opportunity to be with him had passed me by. But what if it hasn't?"

"It has." Bella's voice was gentle but firm. "He's getting married in a little over two weeks."

"I know, I know." Wrenching away from Bella, Ashley edged closer to the bluff's end. "But I'm not sure he even loves her. There's no spark in his eyes when he talks about her, you know? And, Bells, he told me their proposal story, and it's so dull and not really even a proposal, and then he told me how he'd always imagined proposing, and it was in *our* spot."

They'd spent more time there together, on an old blanket staring up at the stars, than anywhere else combined. "Is it so wrong to want him to choose me instead?"

Tears beat against the back of her eyes, burning as she held them in.

From her place behind Ashley, Bella was quiet for a few moments. The roar of the ocean filled in the gaps between them.

At last, her friend approached her, holding out a small bouquet of flowers. "I know you love him, but you can't steal him away. That's not the woman I know and love."

Ashley took the flowers, gripping the stems so tight she thought they might break. "I don't want to be that woman." The sweet smell of the long, skinny flowers wafted up to her nose. "But he's the only one I know who seems to see the real me, and I don't have to do anything for him to do that. He just … does it."

"Oh, Ash. I'm sorry."

"What am I going to do, Bells?" Her voice revealed her anguish, but she didn't care. She had to get this out. "What do I do with this hole in my heart?"

"When I thought I'd lost Ben, I felt the same way." Bella sighed as she looked out across the horizon, where the sun had started its early evening descent. "But if you go after Derek now, you'd be inflicting the same pain on his fiancée. And he might end up resenting you for it later."

Ashley swallowed hard. "You're right. I just need to forget this ever happened. Claire comes back to town in a week and a half. I can survive that long."

"Maybe you should just tell your boss he needs to take over planning this wedding."

"No." It would be bad enough to lose Derek all over again. But to also lose her chance at a new life—one she'd always wanted? That couldn't happen. "I've got this."

Ashley's grip on the flowers loosened, and this time she let them slip away slowly into the sea. The wind took one and spun it around and around in circles before it drifted to its fate.

But flowers didn't die completely, and neither would Ashley. Spring brought new life, after all.

Ashley still had something worth living for. And she wasn't letting it go without a fight.

CHAPTER 11

*D*erek knew when to call in some backup. "So you're going to stay the whole time she's here, yeah?"

Heather rolled her eyes as her hands plunged into the bowl of cookie dough. "I told you I would." She arched an eyebrow at Mia, who sat on the barstool at the white marble countertop coloring a picture of some Disney princess. "Uncle Elephant sure is on edge, isn't he? I wonder why that is."

Mia glanced up and scrunched her nose. "What's 'on edge' mean?"

Derek ruffled her curls. "Nothing, Peanut. Mommy's just reading into things."

Rolling a ball of dough between her hands, Heather pursed her lips. "Am I? I don't ever remember you inviting me—much less begging me—to hang out with you and Ashley before. Something's definitely up."

Walking toward the oven, he peeked inside, inhaling the calming scent of the chocolate chip cookies Heather had set inside only minutes before. "I just thought you'd be able to help us with some wedding stuff. You can stand in for Claire."

"Mm-hmm."

Fine, who cared if Heather believed him? Fact was he absolutely could not allow himself to be alone with Ashley again. That was why he'd invited her out to the vineyard, where he had the home advantage.

The doorbell rang and he pointed at Heather. "I'm counting on you."

She plopped another dough ball onto the cookie sheet. "Even if I leave, Mia will stay if you keep plying her with cookies."

"Cookies are my favorite!"

His niece's sweet giggle brought a smile to Derek's face, sustaining him as he trudged to the front door.

But as soon as he opened the door, his grin disappeared.

Ashley had a death grip on Claire's binder, and her posture was so rigid that an army general would be proud. "Hi."

"Hey." His jaw clenched. "Thanks for coming over on a Saturday night."

"Anything for one of my grooms." Ashley moved past him. "Where did you want to set up?"

"In the kitchen. Heather and Mia are going to keep us company."

Ashley's shoulders sank like a balloon pricked by a pin. "Great idea."

So he wasn't the only one who regretted what had almost happened two days ago. Good. "Glad you approve." He led her through the living room into the kitchen. The rest of the house was quiet tonight, since Dad and Nancy were at a movie and Christina lived in her own apartment in town.

Mia looked up at their arrival. "Miss Ashley!"

Ashley set the binder on the counter and leaned down to hug Derek's niece. "Good to see you, Mia. It's been a while. I wasn't sure you'd remember me."

"I'm four. I have a good memory."

"I should have known better." Ashley's laugh swept through the kitchen. "Heather, whatever you're making smells heavenly."

Heather wiggled her doughy hands. "Nothing special. Just cookies. But you're welcome to them once they're ready." Turning, she washed her hands in the sink, then flicked them dry before snagging a towel. "What are you guys working on tonight?"

"Now that we're holding the wedding at the inn, we've got to figure out decorations. A lot of what we were planning to use was supposed to be provided by the lodge, so I wanted to show Derek some pictures of what was possible and get his final okay to order or rent it." Sliding into one of the six chairs at the rectangle oak table, Ashley opened the binder. "I should be out of your hair in an hour, tops."

"Feel free to stay longer, if you'd like." Heather looked at Derek with a challenge in his eyes.

"Y-yeah." He glared at his sister before turning his attention back to Ashley and joining her at the table. "Stay as long as you'd like."

Ashley studied him. "I have a lot of work to do."

"Oh, but Mia and I were going to go play outside on the deck once I'm done making cookies," Heather said, a little too much saccharine in her tone. "You're welcome to join us. It's supposed to be a lovely night."

He was going to kill his sister.

Mia turned on her stool and bounced where she sat. "Oh yes, Miss Ashley. You have to stay and play. Pretty, pretty please with a cherry on top?"

"How could I refuse such an offer?"

They settled in at the table and worked through the details, Heather piping up with ideas between cookie batches. The chocolate served to loosen them up, and by the end of the night, they were all laughing over memories from their youth.

"My brother was such an idiot sometimes." A wry grin hooked Ashley's lips. "Who in their right mind would try to jump from the roof of a two-story house into the pool?"

"To be fair, probably most teenage boys I knew." Heather wiped away the evidence of four cookies on Mia's face with a wet cloth. Mia yawned.

"Not me." Derek leaned his chair onto its hind legs, his hands looped together around the back of his head. "I told him it wouldn't work."

"Ever the logical one. If only he'd listened to you, he wouldn't have broken his leg." Ashley peeked at the clock. "Oh, I'm sorry. I didn't mean for this to take so long. We just have one more thing to discuss and then I'll be out of your hair."

"Do you have time to take a break now?" Heather kissed Mia on the head. "It's almost this one's bedtime."

Click, click, click. Ashley's thumb was getting a workout with her pen. "Um, sure."

Mia jumped down from her stool and held out her hand to Ashley. "Come on. I'll let you pick any of the Barbies. Except for the wedding Barbie. She's my favorite."

"Oh, she's mine too. But I'm sure I can find a great second favorite." Laughing, Ashley took his niece's hand.

Mia held out her other. "Uncle Elephant. You too. We need a Ken. And you're the best Ken around."

"He really is, isn't he?" Heather squeezed Derek's shoulders. "You've been summoned, big brother."

"All right, all right." Standing, he made his way toward Mia and Ashley, whose eyes laughed at him. He bowed. "Ken, at your service."

Mia's and Ashley's giggles pealed through the lofty kitchen. His niece stole his hand, tugging him and Ashley toward the living room.

He turned to eye Heather. "Aren't you going to join us?"

"After I clean the dishes."

"I can do that later. Come on."

"I'll be right out." Her eyes held a twinkle.

The traitor.

After the three of them had picked out dolls—or, rather, Mia assigned them—they headed to the back door. Stepping out, Mia went straight for the brown swing attached to the underside of the porch roof by two metal chains and plopped down. "Okay, Uncle Elephant, you sit on one side and Miss Ashley on the other."

Both of the adults obeyed the little dictator, and the wood groaned with the effort. Mia proceeded to tell each of them what to say and where to move.

After fifteen minutes of playing with the bride Barbie, she inclined her head toward Ashley. "We can switch dolls now if you want."

"Oh, I kind of like being the doctor Barbie."

Mia frowned. "But the bride Barbie and Ken need to kiss, and Mommy told me I'm too young to make the Barbies kiss. So you have to do it."

Okaaay. Enough of that. "Peanut, you know what I think it's time for?"

His niece eyed him warily. "What?"

"Snuggles and stars."

Her eyes lit up. "My favorite!" Then, after placing all of the dolls gently on the ground, she scrambled up into his lap, leaving a Mia-sized gap between Derek and Ashley.

"Snuggles and stars?" Ashley arched an eyebrow. "What's that?"

"We snuggle and look at the stars, silly." Mia shook her head as if it should have been obvious. "Scoot over so you can snuggle too. It doesn't work if you're too far away."

"Um, I should probably—"

"But, Miss Ashley, you promised you'd stay."

Ashley's eyes met Derek's, and she shifted on the seat.

Ugh. She was uncomfortable. Of course she was, after what he'd pulled on Thursday. "Miss Ashley needs to go."

Then Mia busted out the trembling lower lip. She was a wily one. "But ..."

"All right. I can stay for a few minutes."

"You sure?" He studied Ashley.

Her gaze shifted down to Mia, then back up to him. "Yeah." She moved a bit closer to him on the bench.

He shouldn't be so happy to have her near.

The temperature had dropped rapidly with the sun, and Mia's little body shivered against him, so Derek pulled a quilt off the back of the swing where someone had left it on some previous night. After tugging the quilt over them both, he tossed half of it across Ashley's legs.

"Now, let's look at some stars, shall we?" He pointed out the obvious ones, including Mia's favorite, the Big Dipper. Crickets chirped as the three of them laughed and made up silly stories, Ashley contributing one about Leo, the lion who got his head stuck in a jar of honey.

Eventually, Mia started to yawn and turned to snuggle into Derek's chest. After less than a minute, her breathing evened.

Ashley glanced down from the sky and at the four-year-old. "I think she's out." Her voice remained soft.

"Guess I'm not going anywhere for a while." His chest squeezed as he watched Mia, took in the relaxed peace in her features. "We just had one more thing to talk about wedding wise, right?"

"Oh." Ashley straightened a bit on the seat. "Yes. Vows."

"Vows?"

"Yeah." She coughed. "Do you guys want to go traditional or write your own?"

"I guess I haven't thought much about it."

"Really?" Ashley's hands played with the raggedy fringe on the blue quilt. "Hmm."

"What?" He winced at the sharpness in his tone. Thankfully, Mia didn't wake up. Derek lowered his voice. "What?"

"Nothing."

"I know you, Ash, and that wasn't nothing." The wind kicked up, nipping his face. He adjusted the quilt better around Mia, covering her neck and ears.

"I just …" Ashley heaved out a hard breath and fixed her gaze once more on the sky, where thousands of stars lit the black around them.

That was her—light and beauty even in the darkness.

"You just what?"

"Do you love her, Derek?"

His grip on the quilt tightened, its soft timeworn fabric digging into his hands. "Why are you asking me that?"

"Most couples I work with … they just act differently than you guys do."

"So people have to act all lovey-dovey for you to believe they should get married?"

"No. That's not it." She turned her body toward him, her foot sidling up to his for a moment before it fell away. "You said you know me, but I know you too. And this whole thing just doesn't jibe with the man I know. He was steady and logical, yes, but he was passionate too."

"I can't afford to be passionate now. I have responsibilities." He pressed a kiss to the top of Mia's head. "People counting on me."

"I can certainly understand that, but—"

"If you did, you wouldn't be challenging me on this."

His niece rustled beneath him. Oops. He needed to be better about holding in his temper.

Ashley's eyebrows pulled downward. "I don't get what all of that has to do with you marrying Claire." Her voice hissed across the expanse between them, which might as well have been miles instead of inches. "What I want to know is whether this marriage is really going to make you happy."

"Happy enough."

She threw her hands in the air. "What does *that* mean?"

"It means that even if I don't love her like everyone thinks I should, I'll still be happy." He ground out the words, cringing a bit as Ashley's eyes widened. But it felt good to tell her the truth. Might as well. In fact, he should have done it long before now. "Look, you might not agree, but marrying Claire means security for her family and mine. It'll allow me to save the vineyard."

Silence reigned between them for what seemed like an eternity. Ashley blinked. "You're marrying her because of the vineyard?"

"It's not just the vineyard. It's Dad. Doing this saves him the stress of overwork, which could add years to his life."

Her hand absently stroked Mia's back. "It's very noble of you to want to save your family, but your dad would never be okay with you selling yourself to do it. I've got to assume he has no idea."

"And it's going to stay that way." He sighed. "I appreciate the concern, but I've got this figured out. Partnering with Claire is the only way for us both to get what we want." The irony of saying that to Ashley slapped him upside the head.

Because if he really let himself think about what he actually wanted, what his heart craved ...

"What does she get out of it?"

"She'll inherit her family's vineyard once she's married. Her grandpa isn't well either."

Ashley's hand stilled. "Derek, it's not your job to fix this for your family."

"If not me, then who? You know you'd do the same thing for your family. I figured you, more than anyone, would understand."

"I—"

"After all, you're the one who's sacrificing all her sleep, all her time, for things she doesn't really want."

"That's not true. I'm working hard so I can buy the business from Kyle."

"What about the festival? And the family reunion? And Ben's wedding? Where do those fit into your dream?"

Her eyes flashed. "I just love people. I want to make them happy."

"How's that working out for you, huh? There's a difference between loving people and being a doormat." A tiny sliver of guilt pricked his heart as the words left his lips. "Sorry. That came out harsher than I intended."

"Sounded like exactly what you wanted to say." She stood, her end of the quilt sliding off of her legs. "I am *not* a doormat, Derek Campbell. And I may be overbooked, but at least I'm not so focused on one thing to the detriment of all others."

"The other things don't matter as long as the most important one is taken care of."

"So your heart doesn't matter? What you want doesn't matter?"

"No." He swallowed hard. "They don't."

Mia turned in his arms but stayed asleep.

For the second time that evening, Ashley's shoulders deflated. She pressed her lips together, and her hands became fists at her side. "That's where you're wrong. You're going to wake up someday and realize they matter very much. But by then, it'll be too late."

Pivoting, she walked back inside the house.

And with her exit, the clouds shifted overhead, covering the stars and shrouding the vineyard in darkness.

CHAPTER 12

*T*oo bad cloning machines were not a thing. Because if there were two of her, Ashley might actually have a shot at finishing her to-do list this week.

Kyle would be no help—he was out of town visiting his sister again. Probably keeping the idea of his niece as successor in his back pocket in case Ashley failed miserably.

Which, at this rate? She just might.

Rubbing her temples, she stared at her office computer. The proof for Ben and Bella's invites had finally come through, and she needed to approve it ASAP if there were any chance of getting the invitations delivered in a timely fashion. But when she'd forwarded the email to Bella this morning, her future sister-in-law had texted back that she was in Los Angeles visiting her mom for the day and couldn't see the print very well on her phone and could Ashley double-check the info and get it sent off?

"There's a difference between loving people and being a doormat." Two days later and Derek's words still stung. Things usually hurt the most when they smacked of truth.

Maybe she really shouldn't have said yes to so many things.

Too late now. Besides, given the last-minute nature of the wedding, Ben and Bella's timeline was already tight with the printer. The sooner they turned the proof around, the better.

Enlarging the picture the printer had sent her, Ashley studied the details of the invitation. The font appeared to be the same loopy and formal selection Bella had made and—

"I'm guessing you haven't eaten yet today."

She glanced up to find Shannon in the doorway carrying a personal-size pizza box from Froggies, which her parents owned. "Does half a granola bar count?" Glancing at the clock, she grimaced. How was it three o'clock already? At this rate, she'd be here until ten or eleven, easy.

"Nope." Shannon stepped inside and shut the door behind her. Eyeing Ashley's less-than-pristine desk, she quirked an eyebrow. "Where should I put this?"

"Here." Opening a desk drawer, Ashley swept a stack of files inside. "You're a lifesaver."

After plopping the pizza box onto the now-empty spot, her cousin settled into the chair opposite the desk. "I thought I'd stop by on my way home from work since you weren't at Baker Family Dinner last night. I've missed you."

"I've missed you too. And last night I had to run a twenty-fifth-anniversary party." Truth be told, Ashley had been grateful for the excuse to avoid further questions from Bella after that embarrassing display in the inn's courtyard four days ago. She opened the pizza box, steam puffing against her face as she breathed in the alluring scent of the best pizza on the West Coast. "How was work today?"

"Oh, most of the same." Shannon picked at what looked like a bit of glitter glue stuck to the sleeve of her casual black tunic dress. As a preschool teacher, her clothes had seen much worse. The job suited her perfectly, though. "But you know Noah Robinson?"

Ashley snagged a piece of pizza from the pie and her

stomach rumbled as she bit into it. Aah. Heavenly. "Yeah, of course." One of Shannon's favorite students, the five-year-old had lived with his grandma on the outskirts of town since his mom left early last year.

Shannon tugged on a piece of her hair, her expression somber. "I found out today his grandma, Mary, has Alzheimer's."

"How bad is it?" Ashley reached into her desk and pulled out a napkin from her emergency stash, then wiped her fingertips.

"Her memory's been questionable for a while now, so unfortunately, I'm not all that surprised. But last week there was an incident at the mall." Shannon's face contorted, like she was trying not to cry. "She left him behind in a store because she forgot he was with her. Social services got involved. Mary had a breakdown and got admitted to the hospital for observation."

"Oh, Shan. I'm sorry to hear that. What's going to happen to Noah now?"

"A neighbor with foster certification is watching him while Mary is in the hospital, but after that, I don't know. He doesn't have any other family around. Poor kid looked miserable at school today."

"I'm sure you're a comfort to him, though. A constant."

Shannon got a faraway look in her eye before refocusing. "Anyway. I didn't come by to discuss that. I've been trying to give you your space since I know you're busy. But you aren't answering my calls and texts, and this isn't the first time I've stopped by—but it *is* the first time that you've actually been available." She paused. "Is everything okay? It must be really hard to be the one in charge of Derek's wedding. I know how you felt about him."

The pizza she'd just eaten sank in Ashley's gut. "I'm fine. Really."

"I think you want to believe that, but the fact that we haven't hung out in over two weeks tells me something is going on." Shannon worried her bottom lip. "I talked to Bella last night ..."

Ashley slumped back in her chair. "Did she tell you what happened last week?"

"No, just that she was concerned about you." Shannon leaned forward. "Ash, you can talk to me, you know."

"Oh, I know that. But I don't even know how I feel about everything that's going on."

"With Derek, you mean?"

Ashley nodded.

"You don't have to know. But as I tell my students on a regular basis, sometimes we have to talk things out to understand how we're actually feeling." A smile flitted over Shannon's face. "And then of course I go into why that's a better course of action than hitting or biting."

"Maybe I'd feel better if I bit someone."

They both laughed, but the levity was short-lived. Ashley sighed. "He doesn't love his fiancée, Shannon."

"What do you mean?" Her cousin's nose scrunched in confusion.

Yeah, well, she wasn't the only one.

Ashley told Shannon about her and Derek's conversation-turned-fight the other night at the vineyard. "The thing is, as much as I try not to, I still love him. And there are times when ..." She huffed out a frustrated groan.

"You think he loves you too?"

"Yes!" She paused. "What do I do now? The only thing I can do is keep moving forward, right? Keep planning their wedding even though it's like a knife in the gut every moment I think about it? I don't think I can change his mind. And I shouldn't want to. Maybe he's right. Maybe this *will* save his family's business. Maybe that *is* more important than love."

"You don't really believe that."

"No, but he does. And that could just mean we're too

different to ever work out, anyway." Ashley shut the lid of the box, trapping the unfinished pizza inside. "Maybe I'm in love with the pre-France Derek, and that man is gone."

Before Shannon could think of a reply, Ashley's phone rang. Glancing at the caller ID, she stiffened. It was as if the caller had heard the confession from across the Atlantic.

"I'll let you get that." Shannon stood. "I didn't mean to keep you from your work for so long. But I'm here if you ever want to talk."

"Thanks, cuz. I really appreciate it. Same goes for you."

As Shannon slipped out the door, Ashley forced a smile. No, the caller wouldn't be able to see it, but maybe the gesture would help infuse enthusiasm into her voice. "Hi, Claire. What can I do for you?"

"Ashley, thank goodness. I need your help."

"Of course." Her heart picked up speed at the panic in the other woman's voice. Claire always seemed so put together. "What's wrong?"

"I had plans to return to town later this week, but complications have arisen and I cannot get back until next Monday."

"All right, well, that's okay. Derek and I are taking care of all the details here, so you don't—"

"*Non*, you have not taken care of this detail. My dress, Ashley. They need at least a week for alterations, and I was going to be getting in just under the wire, as you say, but now, it will be impossible. And I cannot have a dress that does not fit, not for my wedding day."

"Oh." That *was* a problem. "All right. Well, I'll try to find another seamstress in town who can do the alterations in a few days' time."

"I suppose that could work, but it makes me nervous." A pause. "What size are you?"

"Me?" The squeak fell from Ashley's lips before she could stop it.

"Yes. We are the same size, I believe. Close enough, anyway. Lucky thing you are tall."

"Wait, what do you mean?" *Please don't be what I think it is.*

The room suddenly felt extra warm.

"You need to go to the boutique and stand in for my alterations. *Oui,* I think that will work."

"No, it might—"

"Thank you, Ashley. You are a wonder. I need to run. Let me know if there are any issues. Au revoir."

Ashley pulled back the phone and stared at it. She really *was* a doormat, and apparently she was the last person in Walker Beach to realize it.

After shooting an email back to the invitation printer approving the proof for Ben and Bella's wedding, she placed a quick call to Brenda's Bridal Boutique. Three hours later, Ashley was headed out the door for an early-evening appointment to get fitted for another woman's wedding dress. Once she walked through the door, the bridal stylist and owner, Brenda, handed her a puffy white garment bag and pointed her toward a fitting room.

Ashley stepped inside and unzipped the bag, pulling back the edges to reveal a gorgeous sheath dress with see-through sleeves, all of it covered in what she guessed was Calais lace. Disrobing, she then shimmied into the tight number, which hugged her upper half and then flowed off her hips into an elegant sweep train that pooled behind her. There was a bit of gaping under the arms, but maybe that would change once she had the stylist button it. Ashley placed a hand over the lace neckline, which revealed more than she'd normally have been comfortable with. But in this case, the effect was less Kim Kardashian and more Kate Middleton.

It wasn't what Ashley would have chosen for herself—probably something strappy, high waisted, and simple—but Claire had chosen well.

Holding up the top part of the dress, Ashley left the changing room. Brenda helped her get buttoned, then directed her to stand on a small round dais ringed with mirrors. Other than her, Brenda, and the seamstress, there didn't appear to be anyone else in the store. Thank goodness, or the Walker Beach rumor mill would be having a field day trying to figure out who Ashley Baker was marrying.

The seamstress came out with a cushion full of pins. Her cat-eye glasses glinted under the bright lights as she got to work straightening out the train.

Ashley swung her hair around the front and looked over her shoulder. Her eyes raked across the dress, which opened to reveal Ashley's bare back.

Claire would look perfect.

Ashley's legs began to tremble as the seamstress tucked and pinned for what seemed like an hour. In the background, the bell over the door rang and she heard Brenda talking to someone. Great. Maybe Carlotta Jenkins and the rest of Walker Beach would have their fill of gossip today after all.

Finally, the seamstress pulled back, her expert eyes assessing her handiwork. She nodded. "You are done. Please remove the dress very carefully."

"Will do. Thanks."

The seamstress turned and clucked. "Are you the groom? Shame on you for looking! It's bad luck, you know."

Ashley whipped around and nearly toppled from the dais. Derek stood off to the side, jaw tight, a tuxedo bag slung over his shoulder. His Adam's apple bobbed.

Ashley ran her hands down the lacy bodice, then stopped as Derek's hypnotic gaze followed the motion.

She forced a laugh. "I'm not sure it counts if he's just seeing the dress, not the bride."

The seamstress lifted an eyebrow as she glanced between

Derek and Ashley. "Could have fooled me." She walked off, muttering to herself.

"What are you doing here?" He strode toward her, stopping at the edge of the dais. For a moment, they were the same height, their faces inches apart.

"Claire asked me to come in for alterations, since we're the same size. No biggie."

"Right." He grunted the word. "No biggie."

Was he mad at her for trying on Claire's dress? They hadn't spoken since their argument on Saturday night, and maybe this was one more thing he'd hold against her. Other feelings aside, she still had to live in this town with him after he was married—assuming he and Claire stayed put.

Ashley lifted the hem of the gown and stepped down. "Hey, I wanted to apologize for the other night. You can marry whoever you want. And as your friend, I should support you. So." She stuck out her hand. "Friends?"

The air crackled as he blinked, like snapping out of some trance.

"Yeah, sure." His fingers closed around her palm. "Friends."

Friends?

Baloney.

He was still in love with Ashley Baker.

The revelation had smacked him like a two-by-four the second he'd seen her in that wedding dress, and he still felt numb from the hit while he stood outside the dressing room as she changed back into her normal clothes and flip-flops.

A stronger man would leave, but he stayed, leaning against the wall. Waiting. He took the opportunity to get his head on straight.

Because, despite his deeper emotions, they *were* friends. Had been for years. Definitely he could choose to focus on that fact.

Probably, at least.

Ashley emerged, eyes bright and hair worn back.

Friends. Friends.

She pulled up short. "I didn't expect you to still be here."

"Thought I could walk you wherever you're going next." He shrugged. "It's dark out." *Real smooth.*

"It's Walker Beach." A smile teased her mouth. "But I appreciate the thought." She headed out the door and he followed, the cool air a welcome relief after the heat he'd encountered in the bridal shop.

Stopping at his Jeep, he tossed his purchased tuxedo inside. With its sharp edges and bow tie, the thing should have made him feel like Double O Seven, but he'd felt like a trussed-up penguin instead. "All right, you don't need me to walk with you. But can I?" Great, he sounded desperate. "I want to apologize."

"Well, if you want to apologize, by all means."

Walking down the sidewalk between the buildings, they emerged onto the boardwalk and turned north. There were plenty of people out for an evening stroll, but not so many that it felt overly crowded. On instinct, he headed for the sand. They removed their flip-flops, hooking them over their fingers as they continued their trek down the beach.

Moonlight reflected off the water, which pulsed onto the shore, lapping at their feet. The wet sand squished between his toes.

"So, about this apology …"

"I was just about to get to that, Miss Impatient."

Her giggles pealed over the water. "Anytime, then."

Derek leaned down and flicked some water up at her.

She shrieked and jogged ahead out of the splash zone.

He caught up. "I shouldn't have called you a doormat, Ash."

Taking a deep breath, he considered his words. "I'm really sorry about that. You're just a much nicer person than I am."

The stars gave enough light for him to catch the soft smile curving on her lips. "As much as I hate to admit it, I think there's some truth in what you said. It's something I'm going to try to work on."

"You don't have to change, Ash. You're perfect just the way you are." Her quick look seared him. Okay, probably not the right thing to say. *Friends, friends.* "We all have areas where we can grow, of course. But maybe I was too quick to judge you."

"You're not the first one to suggest that I may have a failing in my inability to say no."

"Well, like I said. We all have our failings." He grinned at her. "Except for me, of course."

Now the water came flying at him, and he let loose a surprised laugh as the cold hit his face. He had to rein in the impulse to grab her around her waist and fling her into the water. "Watch it."

"Just trying to keep you humble." She laughed, then grew quiet. "Do I have a savior complex, Derek?"

"I thought that was me."

"Maybe it's both of us." Ashley stopped walking and turned to watch the water for a moment. "Seriously, though. I'm always the first one to step up and volunteer if no one else does. I don't refuse anything if someone asks, even when I probably should. Right now I'm swimming in responsibilities and yet if a family member or friend asked me to help them in some way, I'm not sure I could find it in me to say no."

"Like you said, you just love people. Ash, you're one of the most selfless people I know. And that's great. But maybe try putting yourself first sometimes."

"And what exactly would that accomplish?" She walked back up the beach a bit, plopping onto the dry sand.

He joined her, making sure to put a good foot between them. "I don't know. You'd actually get what you want?"

Ashley rubbed her elbows, a faraway look in her eyes. "That's just not how it works for me."

"What do you mean?"

Biting her lip, she glanced at the full moon hovering above them. "Ever since I was a kid, I've known that it's easier to help other people get what they want than to fight for what I do."

"Example?"

She paused for a moment. "Okay. When I was eleven years old, it was my birthday weekend. And you know my mom—she always made a huge deal out of birthdays, letting me and Ben pick our own meals and our choice of activity on our special day." Ashley tugged her knees against her chest. "All I wanted to do was go as a family to see the latest Disney movie at the theater. But Ben was invited to a friend's birthday party, and Dad had something come up with his construction business, and Mom had to help him. She said we'd reschedule, and we did celebrate with pizza and a cake the next weekend, but we never saw that particular movie until it came out on video."

It must have been a powerful memory for her to still talk about it with such resignation in her voice. "That stinks. I'm sorry."

"It's just how it is." Finally, she glanced at him. "Now it's your turn. Why do you feel like you have to fix everything for people?"

"Guess I haven't really psychoanalyzed myself." He paused a beat. "But if I had to hazard a guess, it probably started when Mom left. Dad was a shell of himself for a long time, and the girls were too young to help out, so I just started learning the business and doing what I had to do to get us through."

"Weren't you only nine?"

"Ten." It was so long ago, and yet like Ashley, he recalled certain things with aching clarity. "I remember one time when I was working with the cellar rats, trying to heft this barrel, and I just couldn't do it. As if that wasn't embarrassing enough, I started crying really hard. Jorge found me. He placed his hand on my shoulder, looked me in the eyes, and told me that someday, I was going to be the man of the house. And that, while it was okay to cry in private, I needed to be strong for my sisters."

"What an awful thing to say to a kid whose mom had just left."

He smiled at the way her spine had stiffened in defense of his childhood self. "But he was right. From then on, if I didn't know how to do something, I figured it out. *That* made me strong."

"There's nothing weak about asking for help, you know."

"That's probably something we both need to learn."

"Hmm." She laid her head on her knees, her face turned toward him, lips tipped downward.

And man, what he wouldn't give to turn that frown the other way. To see her light up, the spunky woman he'd always known her to be.

A plan formed in his mind. "I know we don't have a movie theater in town and that I'm not your family and it's not even your birthday. And at the risk of sounding like Mr. Fix It, I'm going to ask you a question. I want you to answer as honestly as possible." He inclined his head toward her. "Ashley Baker, what do you want, right here, right now?"

"What?"

"I mean it." He waggled his eyebrows. "The world is your oyster—which is a terrible metaphor, by the way, because oysters are disgusting."

She laughed, her eyes twinkling. There was that spark. Now to coax it out.

"For real, though. What do you want to do tonight? Call up the old gang for a game night? Go for a run? Hit the theater in San Luis?" Okay, probably shouldn't have suggested that last one—sounded too date-like. "I'll do anything. Whatever you want."

"Anything?" And man, the look in her eyes, the grin curling her lips, had turned slightly wicked.

It was entirely too attractive.

Friends, friends.

"Anything. So what'll it be, Baker?"

"I want to swim."

He couldn't help the laugh bubbling up in this throat. "It's May. Your parents' pool will be freezing."

"No, no, no." She pointed to the ocean. "I want to swim out there."

"You're nuts."

"Chicken?"

Derek scoffed. "Hardly. But it's against the rules to swim after sundown."

"Only if we get caught. Besides, we'll be in and out before anyone notices us."

Derek tilted his head. "Why do you want to do that?"

"I don't know." She fiddled with her earlobe, shoulders deflating a bit. "Forget I said anything. It's dumb and impulsive and—"

"No, no, no." He was definitely going to regret this. "We're doing it."

"Really?"

"Yeah, really." He stood and offered her a hand up.

She tugged him toward the water. "I can't believe you're honestly going to do this."

Her hand felt warm in his. *Friends, friends.*

He forced a smile. "I said I would, didn't I?"

And Derek was a man of his word.

Even when he really didn't want to be.

~

Amazing how a dip in fifty-something-degree water could make a girl feel all warm and toasty inside.

Ashley dried her hair with the beach towel Derek had pulled from the back of his Jeep after their illicit swim. "That was awesome." She sat back against the passenger's seat while heat pumped through the vents. A few empty food wrappers littered the ground at her feet.

He eyed her. "Yes, it was quite refreshing when you chose to dunk me in the frigid ocean."

"You loved it." She snorted at the memory.

He'd come up sputtering, barking with laughter. *"You little—"*

And then he had dived for her. She'd done her best to outswim him, but he was strong, easily catching up and snatching her around her waist before tugging her under. Her eyes had burned from the salt, and her skin had prickled from the cold, but she hadn't felt that alive in a long time.

"It was more fun than I thought it'd be. But only because I got you back."

"Only because I let you." She ran her fingers through her tangled hair. "Now that wasn't so hard to admit, was it? Derek Campbell actually knows how to have fun."

"Shh, don't tell."

"I wouldn't dare."

She studied Derek while he drove the short distance to her office. The stars and moon from outside the windshield illuminated the smooth planes of his forehead, and oh, he was the most handsome man she'd ever known.

Her mouth went dry. "Thanks again for doing that just to make me feel better." She swallowed. "You're a good friend." Because that's what they were.

Friends.

And if she wanted him in her life, she'd have to be content with that.

"Anytime." His hands seemed to tighten around the steering

wheel, but no, Ashley was reading too much into it, projecting her own feelings onto him.

They rode the rest of the way in silence, and by the time his Jeep pulled up to the front, the clock read eight-thirty-two. All Ashley wanted to do was tell him to turn around and take her home instead, but a stack of work a digital mile long called her name. She'd never be able to sleep after that swim anyway—after all the ways it had awakened something in her, something she'd been trying to tamp down since the day Derek had returned.

She turned to him. "Thanks for the ride."

Unsnapping his seatbelt, he reached for his door handle. "Let me walk you in."

"You really don't need to do that."

"I'll make sure no one is inside who shouldn't be." At her quirked eyebrow and what she hoped was a dubious look, he shrugged. "That's what a friend would do, right?"

Why fight it? When Derek got his mind on something, half the time it was better to just go with it. "Okay."

They both climbed out of the SUV and walked up the sidewalk toward the darkened Whimsical Weddings storefront. Ashley snagged her keys from her purse, unlocked the door, and stepped inside.

"You walking ahead of me kind of defeats the purpose of my offer." Derek followed her, then shut the door behind them.

"Sorry to spoil the fun, Rambo, but I don't think there are any bad guys here." Her eyes adjusted quickly to the dark, and she maneuvered to the back where her office was located. Pushing open her door, she flicked on the light.

Ashley turned to invite him back, but ran into his chest instead. "Oomph!" Despite their damp clothing, heat radiated from him.

"Sorry." She pulled away, fleeing to the safety of her desk chair.

"No worries." He stood in the doorway, half in the room, half out. "I guess everything is okay here. I'll just go."

"Okay." Her heart ached with fullness—so much she wanted to say but couldn't. "Thanks again."

"Anytime." There was that word again, but it wasn't true. In just under two weeks, he'd marry Claire, and then there would be no more "anytimes." At least not for Ashley.

"I'll see you later." As if on autopilot, her fingers moved to her mouse and she forced her attention onto her computer screen. Several emails sat unread. One caught her eye, and she clicked it open, scanning it quickly. "Wait a second. Can you come to take a look at this?"

Derek rounded the desk and leaned down just over her shoulder to look at the screen. He smelled like fresh breezes and salt and ... danger. "What is it?"

"This is the music setlist the DJ just sent over. Would you mind making sure there's nothing you want to ax or add?"

"I don't mind."

"Great." She waited a split second, then eased out of the chair. "Here. Sit."

They exchanged places, and she paced while he looked over the Excel document. After a few seconds, he looked up. "I don't know half of these songs."

"Really?" Made sense, actually. Derek had always been a classic rock kind of guy. "Like what?"

"I don't know." He pointed to the screen. "Like this one. 'Happy' by Pharrell Williams? Sounds kind of childish."

"Oh, that one's fun. It was on the radio all the time when it came out."

His lost look and shrug made her giggle. She pulled her phone from her purse and navigated to one of her music apps. "Here, I'm sure you've heard it." After she found the song and hit Play, the peppy beat pumped throughout the small room. Ashley lifted her hands in the air and swayed her hips to the music. "Ringing any bells?"

"Nope. Sorry." But he didn't look sorry. He looked amused, his lips twisted in a grin, eyes laughing at her.

"You're hopeless." Ashley kept moving. "How can you sit there when this fun song is playing?"

"I'm having a lot of fun just watching you."

With a laugh, she yanked him out of the chair. "Too bad. Come on. Show me your best moves."

"Ash, you're crazy. I don't dance."

She pretended to hold a fake microphone and sang into it, still bouncing, one arm lifted in the air like she was a gospel singer. "Dude, you're getting married soon and there will be dancing. You've got to figure it out."

"The only move I know is the shopping cart."

"I'm sorry, the what?"

"You know." He held his arms straight out and waist high, walking in place. Then he reached one arm up at a time, pretended to grab something on an imaginary shelf, and threw it down. "The shopping cart."

Ashley folded in half with laughter. "That's the best thing ever." Then she straightened. "But can you do the sprinkler?" Placing one hand behind her head and the other straight out, she pulsed the second arm around in a half circle.

Now it was Derek's turn to guffaw. "You look ridiculous."

They alternated dance moves until the song ended, slinking into a soft ballad randomly chosen by the music app on her phone.

Ashley's ribs ached from laughing. "You're a natural."

"Yeah, well." Derek leaned back against the desk, cheeks red. His black T-shirt had mostly dried by now, but the ends of the sleeves still clung to his biceps. "I'm not quite sure that's the kind of dancing I should do at the wedding."

The wedding.

Like the waves from earlier this evening, reality crashed back in. Ashley sucked in a ragged breath, then coughed. "You'll be fine." A beat. "I could teach you."

Eek. Why had she said that? That was a very bad idea. Worse than swimming in freezing cold water with a former flame.

Derek pushed off the desk, advancing a step toward her. "You want to teach me to dance?"

Ashley found herself nodding. "I mean, I don't have to. But it's not really that hard." A nervous chuckle bubbled up from her chest. "You just put your arms around each other and sway. Nothing to it."

He drew closer, encircling her waist with his strong arms. "Like this?" His voice was low, throaty.

Their gazes collided, and her whole body flooded with want for him, needing him.

Needing to feel his lips on hers.

Needing to belong to him.

But *she* didn't belong to him. Claire did.

Then again, she'd never seen him look at Claire the way he was looking at her right now.

"Mm-hmm." She looped one arm around his neck. The other hand found its way to his cheek. Slowly, she trailed her traitorous fingers over his beard, the bristles like tiny needles against her skin.

"Ash."

She froze, sensing the serious nature of his tone. She'd gone too far. Ashley started to drop her hand, but he caught it and gently placed it back where it had been.

Ashley swallowed hard. "Yeah?"

"Then what do we do?" A pause, a searching of her eyes. "Sway?"

At her nod, he started to move them in a circle. The slow music poured from the phone, encouraging them on. Ashley's nerves fired in every direction, her heart pitching against her chest in a rhythm at least twice as fast as the song.

Derek's arms tightened around her waist, pulling her closer. "You're a good friend, Ashley."

She stopped moving, dropped her arms, withdrew, the back of her legs now pressing against the desk. The palms of her hands found the top of the desk as she sat on the very edge. The movement grounded her.

Friends.

Right.

He closed the gap between them once more, leaning down, close. "I've been thinking about what you said. About how I shouldn't marry someone without loving them." Moving his head to the left, Derek's lips now hovered above her ear. His warm breath puffed against her lobe, tickling her, making her shiver. "About how I'll regret it forever." His mouth grazed the middle part of her ear.

What was he saying?

He drew back his head again, looking down at her, and licked his lips. "I can't think with you so near."

"So stop thinking." Instantly, she regretted the words. They were too bold, even if she'd been someone who was used to asking for what she wanted.

But then Derek swooped in and kissed her, and Ashley's whole body caught fire. A guttural moan bubbled up from her chest as his mouth burned a trail from her lips to her cheek to her ear to the curve of her neck. Both her arms hooked around him again and their mouths found each other once more, giving and taking in equal measure. Ashley pushed her hands through the sides of his hair, her fingers massaging the back of his head as she deepened the kiss. Pulling back slightly, she nipped at his ear. He growled with pleasure before turning his head and catching her lips again.

Finally, they stopped. Both of them huffed air in and out,

and the most delicious warmth curled through her as she laid her head against his chest. "I love you, Derek Campbell."

He didn't say anything at first, and reality dawned as the music in the background shifted once more—this time to something dark, foreboding.

She risked a glance up at him, and the pain in his gaze was enough to tear her in two.

"Ash."

Shaking her head, she closed her eyes for only a moment. "Don't say it."

He took a step back.

Her hands flew to the desk once more for support, and the edge bit into her fingers. She gripped tighter, welcoming the pain.

"I'm sorry." His ragged whisper sliced into her resolve.

But no, she wasn't going to go down without a fight. Not now. Not after *that*. "Don't do this, Derek. Don't walk away."

He scrubbed a hand down his face. "I have to."

"Why?" She had a right to know that much—why he'd kissed her and why he was willing to toss aside the possibility of a life together.

"The vineyard ..." He looked away.

"I just told you I love you, and all you can talk about is the vineyard?"

"I—I can't just forget about the vineyard."

"Then why did you kiss me?"

"That shouldn't have happened. I was so determined to just stay friends. I can't believe ..." He groaned.

"Why. Did. You. Kiss. Me?" She surged forward and pushed against his chest. He didn't budge. She pushed again. And again. Hot tears coursed down her cheeks.

"I'm sorry." His hands curled into fists. "You deserve better than this." Then, with one final look of apology, of torment, he turned and left her alone.

Ashley hooked her arms around herself.

Unbelievable.

Except, not really. Because she'd been right all along.

No matter how hard she fought for it, Ashley Baker never really got what she wanted.

CHAPTER 13

*T*he day had finally come for Derek to pay the piper.

Because Claire was returning to Walker Beach.

Derek grunted as he hefted a case of Zinfandel onto his shoulder. The smell of the loamy cellar grounded him as he walked toward the exit.

Mateo stopped his conversation with a few workers and jogged over. "That's not your job, Boss. Let one of my guys handle it."

"It's fine." The edge of the wood bit into his flesh. "I need a distraction."

"Wedding jitters, eh?" His cellar master's mouth curved into a knowing grin. "I remember feeling that way when I got married. All will be well come Saturday night."

If the wedding even still happened. He hadn't yet informed Claire about the kiss with Ashley a week ago. Had told himself it was a discussion they should have in person. But in reality, he just hadn't had the guts.

He was a coward, afraid that one error in judgment, one moment of pleasure, of finally giving in, would cost his family their futures.

And he was a cad too.

Nodding, he muttered a goodbye to Mateo and maneuvered past him out into the cheery sunlit day. He trudged through the rows of vines. The spring flowering had been steady-going, and within a week or two, young clusters should start appearing. Derek always loved seeing the evidence of an entire half-year of work come to fruition before his eyes. It was predictable, rewarding for those who stayed the course.

If only the rest of life could be that way.

He reached the tasting room and shop, a building about a hundred yards from their house. A few cars sat in the parking lot, fairly normal for a Monday afternoon.

Derek let himself in the back door to the storage room and set the case of wine down. Then he started to unpack the Zinf, placing it in racks where Heather could easily grab what she needed.

Strands of jazzy music drifted back from the front of the house, and he heard muted voices, the occasional laugh. The noises grated against his need for peace.

"Don't we pay someone else to do that?"

Derek glanced up to find his youngest sister in the curved doorway. "Why does everyone keep asking me that? This is our family's vineyard. I'm part of the family. So I can help anywhere I choose."

"Bite my head off, why don't you." Heather's heels clicked on the tile as she advanced. "You're getting married in five days. Shouldn't you be a bit less cranky?"

"Everyone's entitled to a bad day."

"Try a bad week. You've been an absolute bear." Heather pulled one of the bottles from the nearly empty crate at Derek's feet, examining the label. "Why is that? What happened?"

What *had* happened? How had he so utterly lost control? One minute, they'd been laughing like the friends he was deter-mined to be. The next he was holding Ashley close, rationalizing that he was simply learning to dance. Of course, if he'd really wanted to learn, he could have just asked Claire to teach him. Or Heather. Or any number of people except the woman he loved.

Loved.

Man, he was in trouble.

Heather stood there, eyebrows lifted, waiting for his answer.

He removed the last bottle from the case and slid it into the rack, then stacked the crate on top of several others in the corner. "Nothing happened. Everything is how it should be." Or, it would be as soon as he cleared the air with his fiancée. He turned to leave.

"Bro."

He glanced back at Heather, who had a contemplative look on her face. "Yeah?"

"Don't be like me. Don't settle for less than you deserve."

Derek knew without asking that she spoke about Mia's father. To this day, Heather had refused to tell anyone his identity, only that it had been a short-lived mistake that had resulted in a blessing.

But broken-hearted as his sister had been when the whole thing went down, Heather's situation was nothing like his. "I've gotta go." Claire would be here any minute—she'd insisted on renting a vehicle at the airport—and he smelled like sweat and dirt. Might as well be clean when he came clean.

As he showered in his cabin, he soaked in the warmth of the water, so different from the fateful dip in the ocean he'd taken a week ago. Cutting off the stream flowing from the showerhead, he pushed away the piercing guilt he'd felt in leaving Ashley alone in that office. He should have been a man about it. Talked it through. Apologized even more.

But he hadn't trusted himself. Enclosed with her in that small room that smelled of her pineapple and coconut perfume, all alone, after that kiss—who knew what he would have done if he'd stayed?

"Derek?" A delicate knock sounded on the bathroom door. "Are you decent?"

Claire.

"Be right out." He stepped from the shower, steam lingering in the tiny bathroom as he toweled off and pulled on a pair of basketball shorts and a T-shirt.

Time to see if he could fix the mess he'd made.

Emerging into the hallway, he trudged to the living room, where Claire sat on the edge of the couch perusing her phone. A gas fire flickered in the stone fireplace across from her, and the wooden accents in the rustic-but-modern cabin gave the place a cozy flare.

At his approach, Claire stood and walked over. "Hello, *mon cher*." She kissed both of his cheeks, then pecked his lips.

He shouldn't have let her do that, not until he'd made his confession.

"Hey." A squeeze to her waist, and then Derek led her back to the deep-brown couch. "How was your flight?" With her smooth hair and bright red lips, he'd never have known the woman was just on a plane for twelve hours straight.

"Well enough." She nestled her hand inside his, running her fingers down the lines of his palm. "And how are you? I'm so sorry you've had to bear the burden of planning this wedding alone."

"I'm good." He shifted, breathed in through his nose. It was now or never. "But—"

"Grand-père, I am sorry to say, will not be able to attend the wedding. He is so disappointed but sends his best wishes for our health and happiness." Her hand stilled. "I'm sorry I've been so unavailable lately. Things have been busier than I thought they'd be at the vineyard."

As if she should be the one apologizing to him. "I can definitely relate to that."

She leaned toward the hand-carved wooden coffee table and picked up a green to-go cup from Java's Village Bean he hadn't noticed before now. Probably her daily late-afternoon Earl Grey. Claire took a delicate sip before turning her eyes upon him once more. "I realize that in all the rush of planning the wedding, we have not decided what to do after the fact. Which seems to be a bit of an oversight, *oui?*"

"You mean where we'll live?"

"That, among other things." She bit her lip. "Derek, I do not even know if you want children."

Good thing he didn't have a drink or he'd have spewed it everywhere. He hooked a hand behind his head and scratched the base of his skull. "Uh, yeah. I don't know." Not like he *hadn't* thought about that part of marriage, necessarily, but Claire was right—they'd never discussed if they'd keep their relationship strictly business or not. Or what life looked like after the wedding and the inheritance came through. The engagement, everything, had happened so quickly.

Claire's eyebrows scrunched together as she placed a hand against Derek's chest. "I like you very much and respect you, Derek. You know this. I am attracted to you, and I would not mind having that sort of relationship. But ..." Her eyes searched his. "I need to know what *you* want."

"I kissed Ashley."

The words slipped out before his horrified brain could catch up.

Eyes wide, Claire reared back, dropping her tea to the floor.

Derek rushed to pick it up before it could spill onto the wood floor, setting it upright on the table. Then he folded his hands together, leaning forward in his seat. His hands smelled like bitter oranges. "I'm sorry, Claire. That's not how I'd intended to tell you that."

His fiancée's hand drummed against her lips before she stood and paced to the window. "Why did this happen?"

"I was an idiot. And weak. And I'm sorry." Should he join her at the window or give her space? Even after knowing Claire for more than a year, he had no clue what she needed from him in this moment. "It only happened once. And I haven't seen her since."

Claire remained silent, lips pursed.

He had to fight for this marriage. It was all he had left—and he was not so selfish as to realize that his actions had messed with Claire's future, her ability to help her family, as well.

Derek rose and approached the window until he stood next to her. "I know our relationship might not be based on a deep romantic love, but it *is* based on mutual trust, which I've broken. I promise if you just give me another chance, I'll never even look at another woman. You will be my priority, my wife in every way that you want to be."

"You still love her, don't you?"

It was his turn to be quiet. What good would it do to tell her the truth? But he couldn't lie.

"I'll take that as a yes." Claire laid her head against Derek's arm as they stared out the window at the rolling foothills. "Derek, there is something I must tell you as well."

"What's that?"

"While I was home, Sébastien showed up at my office."

"Your ex?"

"*Oui.*" Claire sighed. "He'd heard I was getting married. Told me how sorry he was for leaving me, that it was the biggest mistake of his life. That he still loved me." The words seemed to get stuck in Claire's throat. She coughed. "Of course, I told him he was too late, that love could not possibly be reborn after so much heartache."

See? Claire had been loyal to him. Why hadn't he done her the same courtesy? "Was it painful to see him?"

"Yes. More than I thought it would be." She worried her lip. "And now that I see you, loving Ashley still, even after all this time, after all the heartache she brought you, I wonder if maybe I was too hasty in my reply to him. Maybe love *is* real. Maybe it *can* last, with a little forgiveness and a lot of grace."

Stepping back, Claire squeezed Derek's arm. "Maybe we were both wrong about love."

He cast his eyes downward, their gazes connecting. What was she saying? "Some things are more important than being happy. Isn't that what we've said?"

"*Non.* I never said my life with you wouldn't be happy. But if that is how you have always felt, I could never allow you to bind our lives together. It would be a prison for you."

"That's not what I meant."

"Oh, I know you do not mean to be callous." And then a smile teased her lips. How could the woman beam like that right now? "It was different when we were two people choosing the same path together. But your heart has chosen differently. And, I think, mine has as well. At the very least, it wants to, for the first time in a long time."

Whoa. Derek turned and slumped against the wall beside the window. "So where does that leave us?"

"I'm sorry to say I cannot marry you."

"But what about the vineyards? Our businesses?" He glanced at her.

Claire's small nose scrunched. "I do not know how my grandfather will react to this news about our broken engagement. He may choose to disinherit me because he cannot trust me. I pray that is not the case, but ..."

"Blame it on me, then. It's my fault, after all."

"*Non*, this is my decision too. We will both face our futures with heads held high." She lifted her hand to his cheek, thumb stroking his beard, clear affection written all over her face.

"They may not hold what we thought they would, but maybe, with love, we can really conquer all."

He couldn't help but laugh. "Listen to you, sounding like a romance novel."

She stuck out her tongue in a most un-Claire-like way. "I do not know what is happening to me. I feel like a fool, and yet, a happy one. Do you?"

His heart thumped harder at the question. Because, wait. What did this mean?

If he and Claire were no longer engaged, there was nothing stopping him from pursuing Ashley. True, he didn't have a way to save the vineyard, but the only option he'd had was off the table. That was a problem for another day.

"A fool?" Shaking his head, he leaned in and gave Claire a soft kiss on the cheek. "That about sums it up."

Yeah, he'd be a fool for love.

Pretty sure he'd do anything for Ashley Baker.

CHAPTER 14

*F*ive more days and her agony would be over.

Ashley gripped the railing on the upper deck of the Iridescent Inn, raking her eyes across the waves as they crashed against the shore just beyond. A few guests lounged in the chairs to Ashley's far right, chatting and sipping lemonade. An older couple walked the courtyard, their pace slow, their smiles visible even from her spot above them.

Any moment now, Derek and Claire would show up for a final walk-through of the venue—well, Claire's first walk-through. Supposedly, she'd returned to town yesterday, though Ashley hadn't heard a word from her. After a long day of travel, she'd probably been asleep the moment she climbed into bed.

As for Ashley, her sleep over the last week had only totaled twenty hours, maybe thirty.

Today the weather had the decency to agree with her emotions. Wind whipped her hair across her shoulders and dark clouds marred the blue on the horizon. A storm brewing.

Maybe it would bypass Walker Beach altogether—but that was likely wishful thinking.

"Ben told me I could find you here."

Briefly, Ashley closed her eyes, pinching her nose between her thumb and forefinger. She could do this. She'd simply pretend Derek was any other groom—not the only one she'd ever begged to leave the bride so *she* could have him instead.

"Don't do this, Derek. Don't walk away." Her cheeks flamed at the memory.

She opened her eyes, inhaled, and turned with the same smile she'd wear at a funeral. "So glad you both could—"

Derek stood in front of her, hands shoved into the pockets of his jeans, his deep purple Campbell Wines polo shirt bringing out the chocolate in his eyes.

She squinted past him. "Where's Claire?"

"She's not coming."

"Oh." Why hadn't they called Ashley beforehand? The whole point of this meeting was so Claire could approve their choices for the placement of decor, chairs, et cetera. "Did she tell you when she'd like to reschedule this appointment? I don't feel comfortable making the final decisions without her here."

"Ash." He took a step forward.

Her back pressed against the wood, and just like that, they were back in her office, in those moments she couldn't get out of her head no matter how hard she'd tried. Sleep only brought them out even more vividly in dreams. Working on Derek and Claire's wedding details didn't help. The only thing that would help was getting past this Saturday and then starting her new life as a business owner.

Ashley maneuvered around him, finally able to breathe again. She started walking the length of the decking so Derek hopefully wouldn't notice the way her hands shook.

"Ashley Baker."

Her feet halted and Ashley pivoted.

Derek hadn't moved.

She sighed. "Yes?"

"Claire isn't coming because I'm not marrying her."

Ashley froze. Blinked. Slipped down onto the nearest padded chaise lounge. "What?"

"Are you okay?" In a flash, Derek was there, squatting in front of her, taking her hands in his, eyes roving her face as if worried she might faint.

"I …" Ashley shook her head. "I must have misheard you."

"You didn't."

A light sprinkle started to fall from the sky.

"I don't understand." Her hands felt warm in his, and yet it was wrong. All wrong.

Wasn't it?

"Claire called off the wedding yesterday. But I'm glad she did."

That didn't make any sense. "Why would you be glad? What about the vineyard?"

His half-hearted shrug, the slight tightening of his face, the way he squeezed her fingers—all of that told her more than words ever could. He hadn't fully processed what this would mean for his family.

And it was all Ashley's fault, because she was the worst wedding planner in the history of wedding planners. "I'm sorry."

Everything—including the two of them—was getting wetter by the minute. The guests sitting down the deck a ways stood and headed inside.

"This isn't on you."

Ashley rubbed her chest. "How can you say that? If I'd never offered to teach you how to dance …" Her gaze collided with the ground. Fat drops of rain now beat the decking, turning more urgent by the second.

Yet neither of them moved.

"Look at me."

She refused. Not this time.

But ever so gently, he tilted her chin up so their eyes met. "Claire and I didn't call off the wedding because of the kiss."

"You didn't?"

He frowned. "Okay, technically, we did, but that's ... it's hard to explain."

Her now-drenched clothes hung heavy on her frame. "Can you try?"

Blowing out a breath, he moved to sit next to her on the lounge. "You know I'm not good at saying how I feel. But I guess Claire saw something in me. Something that I'd been trying to hide from myself."

Did he mean ...? Ashley shifted her body sideways so her knees snugged against his. "And what's that?"

Cold water bit at the tops of her legs, but she had to stick this out. Had to allow herself to make it through the storm, to see what peace might lie on the other side.

She rubbed her hands up and down her legs in an attempt to stay warm.

His fingers settled on top of Ashley's, halting her movement. "That I care about you. More than I should for a guy who is marrying someone else."

Her lips parted. Something deep inside her had always known it, had hoped that his feelings went deeper than the physical attraction between them, but he'd never actually said it. And then, it had only been that one time, on the trail by the Moonstone Lodge, and only in reference to his past feelings.

Even then, he'd never said the L-word—just that he'd been "crazy about" her.

What, exactly, did that mean to him?

He angled his head toward hers, their noses millimeters from touching. "Say something."

The rain had started to let up, the sun peeking from behind the cloud cover. And yet, some clouds remained, some water still fell, albeit softer than it had before.

"I don't know what to say. When you walked away the other night, I … I can't tell you how much that hurt."

"I'm so sorry for that, Ashley, but you knew it was wrong too."

"You're right." Alongside the rejection, shame over what they'd done to Claire had settled firmly in, choking Ashley until she'd relinquished all right to feel hurt by his actions. "But then, when days passed, and you didn't call or text or … anything … I knew you were lost to me forever. And now you're saying—well, I'm not even sure what you're saying."

"Then, let me make it perfectly clear." Derek placed a hand on her cheek. "I want to explore this thing between us more, this something that has always been there. I want to take you on a date. Yes, I'm saying it, a real date. And I really want to kiss you. Would that be okay?"

Her heart still ached, joy mingling with the lingering pain. But this was what she'd wanted, right?

"Yes." She gnawed her bottom lip. "That would be okay."

He leaned down, brushing his mouth against hers with the sweetest promise of what was to come.

All too quickly, he pulled back. "Now, about that date. Are you free tonight? I'm thinking we're a bit overdue for dinner together at Mimosa's."

She fiddled with the bottom button on his polo, her insides vibrating. "I think that can be arranged."

What did a woman wear to the first date she'd been dreaming about for years?

Ashley studied the pink dress on the hanger in front of her. Her nose wrinkled as she pushed it down the closet's rack, grabbing for the next hanger. Hmmm. The green blouse was cute and flirty, but she'd had it for years.

A knock sounded from her front door. Who would be stopping by on a Tuesday afternoon?

She eyed herself in the bedroom mirror, grimacing at her ratty T-shirt and cutoff leggings. If it were Derek, he was super early and she'd turn him away. After careening down the hallway, she stopped to squint through the peephole. Madison stood there with a drink carrier and a white bag.

Ashley opened the door. "What are you doing here?"

Her friend held up the bag, which was stamped with the Frosted Cake's logo. "I thought you could use some reinforcements."

"You or the food?"

"Both." Her friend stepped inside the apartment and kicked the door closed.

"Then I guess I shouldn't tell you that I don't think I could eat a thing." Ashley placed a hand against her tight stomach before snatching the drink carrier. "But I *will* take this."

She lifted out the caramel macchiato and took a refreshing sip. The espresso infused strength into her veins. "Bless you."

"That's what friends are for." Madison set the bag on the kitchen table, which sat not too far from the door. "I'm just glad that the library closes early on Tuesdays. And that you actually texted me. I haven't heard from you in weeks."

"That's not true." Ashley turned on her heel and marched back toward her bedroom.

Madison followed. "Maybe not weeks, but it's definitely been a hot minute."

They entered the bedroom and both plopped onto the edge of the queen-sized bed. "I've—"

"Been busy. I know." Madison snatched the carrier from Ashley, plucking her drink from inside. "But this text today— *Derek isn't getting married and we're going on a date tonight*—I mean, what am I supposed to do with that? It tells me none of the juicy details that good friends are entitled to. So spill."

Ashley put her drink on her side table and flopped onto her back. "I don't even know where to start."

"I'm personally a fan of the beginning."

"You're hilarious." Ashley caught her friend up on everything that had happened since the last time they'd spoken. Her eyes followed the dusty ceiling fan blades, which squeaked a bit as the fan rocked on its axis above them. "I've been thinking and rethinking over what he said, how he said it, and even though I said I loved him—which is so embarrassing, by the way—he still hasn't said it to me."

Madison repositioned herself to lean back against Ashley's headboard. "You said he's slow to confess how he feels about stuff. Maybe he loves you too and is waiting for the right time to tell you."

"Maybe." Ashley sat up and played with a loose thread on her sky-blue duvet. "When he told me he wanted to explore what was between us, part of me was ecstatic. But the other part was like, I don't *need* to explore it. I already am sure of it. And I want him to be sure of it too."

"Evan was sure about me before I was sure of him. Sometimes it just takes the other person a while to catch up." A small smile flitted across Madison's mouth. "And now, I can't imagine loving anyone more than I love him."

"I know I should just be grateful for this chance between us, but I still feel super guilty over the way it happened. And what about his vineyard?"

"Sounds like he will have to figure that one out. It isn't up to you to fix it. And like you said, he never would have been happy with that arrangement."

"I guess." Ashley sighed. "There's also a very small sliver of doubt embedded in my heart. I wonder if I'm just a rebound because Claire really did break his heart. What if I'll always love him more than he loves me? All of these questions just keep pinging around in my head."

"Ash, no. You have to stop thinking like that. If what you say is true, he was only with Claire to save his family's vineyard."

"That's what he said." Groaning, she rubbed the corners of her eyes. "Maybe I just shouldn't go tonight. Give it some time. I mean, what will people think of me when they see me out with a guy who was just engaged?"

"People will always find something to gossip about, believe me. Just go on this date, keep talking this out. Tell him what you're thinking, what you're afraid of." Madison stood and tugged Ashley to her feet. "But before you do any of that, you need to change. I may not be very fashionable, but I do know that you don't wear *that* to Mimosa's."

Ashley gave a dry chuckle. "Okay, okay. You're right." Shoving her doubts aside, she and Madison perused her closet like two preteens before a school dance.

After they'd narrowed down the selections to two outfits, Ashley's phone rang. She walked to her nightstand and picked it up, smiling. "Hey, Bells. I have some fun news to—"

"The invitations." Her friend's tone was clipped. "They're wrong."

"What?"

"I thought you proofed these. But the date on them says July thirteenth, not third."

Ashley sank onto the edge of her bed. "I don't—"

"I know I said I wouldn't be a bridezilla, but even I have my limits. The email the printer sent was wrong, which means that either you didn't look closely enough or you told them to make the change and they didn't. Which is it?" Bella's voice shook. "Ashley, this was the one detail that I actually cared about."

The weight of the bed shifted as Madison sat down.

Ashley raked a hand through her hair, tugging when she reached the ends. "I don't know how this happened, Bella." Ashley mentally retraced her steps, trying to remember when she'd proofed the invitations. But everything blended together. "I'll fix it. I promise."

"How? I have almost two hundred invites with the wrong date. And they need to go out this week."

"I'll call the shop, get it fixed."

"They won't reprint them for free when it was our mistake."

She said "our," but she really meant Ashley's. And she was right.

"Just let me worry about that. I'll keep you posted." Ashley said a few more soothing words, then hung up. "I have to fix this."

Madison squeezed her knee. "Anything I can do to help?"

"Thanks, but no. I'll call the print shop and pray they'll do me a solid. I've worked with Raul on several weddings, so there's a chance they'll do the rush order. But it sounds like it was my error. I'll probably have to pay at least a percentage of it."

She whipped her phone out, navigated to her email, and found the proof from the print shop. And sure enough, there it was—an extra one in front of the three. "How did I not see this?" But she knew. She'd been too distracted with Derek, with the Christmas festival, with every other thing she'd committed to.

And now she'd quite possibly ruined her brother's wedding. At the very least, Bella had lost all faith in her. She'd never heard her future sister-in-law talk to anyone the way she'd just talked to Ashley—such tightness and command in her voice. Such anger. Such disappointment.

Ashley couldn't let her down. "I've got to make this call."

"I'll show myself out." Madison stood, then studied her. "What about your date?"

Right. The date. "This is more pressing right now. Derek will understand if I need to be a little late."

Madison thumbed her ear, nose scrunched. "Couldn't you

wait until tomorrow to deal with this? It's already four-forty-five. The print shop is probably closing soon anyway."

"No, I'd just be worried about it all night. Hopefully it'll be a quick conversation and then I can get over to Mimosa's." Her stomach lurched at the thought of having the tough conversation with Derek about where they each stood. But she couldn't stand him up again—not after last time. She'd face whatever was between them head-on.

"Okay." But doubt crept into Madison's tone.

"It'll be fine." Ashley gave her friend a quick hug. "Derek has waited this long for our date. He can wait a little longer."

CHAPTER 15

She hadn't shown up.

Again.

Derek slumped against the back of the stone bench, fingers still locked around the bouquet of flowers he'd purchased from Fleur de Lee this afternoon. The purple blooms—which Lee Rivas had assured him stood for love, depth, and loyalty—had wilted during Derek's two-hour wait.

He checked his phone again. Make that three hours.

By now, Main Street was mostly deserted, and Mimosa's had just closed. He needed to stop lingering, but some stupid part of him still believed she'd show up. He'd give her a few more minutes. After all, she'd said it was a work emergency keeping her away. He understood that. Knew from experience that little fires could grow beyond control very quickly.

But on tonight of all nights, with their history—well, no one could blame a guy for wondering if that were the real story.

Derek's phone vibrated in his hand. His heart skipped as he saw the sender and nearly stopped when he read her message. *I'm so sorry to do this, but I just don't think I can make it tonight. Can we reschedule?*

Yep. He definitely should have called it sooner than this. Should have known this was how it would go. Should have accepted the fact that the past was bound to repeat itself.

But like a fool, he'd believed Ashley when she'd texted initially and said she'd be an hour late. Then again when she'd pushed him off another thirty minutes. And another. And another.

The storm from earlier had cleared, leaving the air crisp and new. He'd thought it a sign of what was to come between them. Now, with every breath, the cold bit into his lungs, slicing through his heart.

Jumping up, he shoved his phone into the pocket of his dress slacks and hurled the flowers into the trash can next to the bench. Derek climbed into his Jeep and started it up, flexing his fingers against the steering wheel as he contemplated his next move. Going home was the obvious choice, but that would mean an entire night of waiting, of torturing himself with the what-ifs.

Forget it. He had to know if he'd tossed away his chance to save his family's vineyard for nothing.

Derek threw the car into Drive and headed toward Ashley's apartment. Once he arrived, he marched up the stairs to her door and knocked, wincing at the way his pounding resounded through the hallway. It was late and a weekday night, after all. But he stood his ground.

After an agonizing minute, the door opened. Ashley stood in the doorway dressed in pajama bottoms and a spaghetti strap shirt, her hair pulled back—looking for all the world like she'd enjoyed a relaxing evening in, not racing around town like she'd claimed.

"Derek? H-hey."

Above him, a fluorescent light flickered. "Can I come in? Or are you busy?" He swallowed hard before anything more forced its way out.

She blew out her cheeks, then released the air as she widened the door. "I'm not busy."

Not waiting for her to change her mind—she seemed to like to do that—he tromped into her apartment. The whole place smelled like a tropical fruit basket and set his nerves on fire.

Turning, he planted his feet wide and crossed his arms. "If you didn't want to go out, you could have just said so."

"You're all dressed up. Did you ..." Her cheeks paled. "Did you actually go to the restaurant? I thought I texted you before you would have left."

"I had a few stops to make before dinner so I left early." No way was he telling her about that wasted bouquet of flowers— or the little stop at the jewelry store he'd made. Just to peruse.

Idiot. Idiot. Idiot.

He swept his arm around the apartment. "How long have you been home?"

"I don't know." She touched the base of her neck. "Thirty minutes?"

"And you didn't think to call me on your way home to tell me you were standing me up?"

Edging past him, she moved to her kitchen counter and took a sip from a pink mug. Guess she'd had time to do a lot of things before texting him five minutes ago. "I figured you'd have given up on me by then."

If only he had.

If only he'd kept his feelings hidden—from himself, from Claire, from Ashley. If only he'd done a better job of keeping his head on straight in the first place. At least with Claire, he'd known what he was getting.

"I'm sorry, Derek. I can only imagine what you thought. What you think."

"It's fine. No big deal. People get stood up all the time." Ignoring her wince, Derek turned to leave.

"Wait. Let me explain."

He stopped, rotated, and leaned with one foot bracing him against the wall. "Okay." Not that he really wanted to hear her excuses.

Ashley tried to hide a yawn behind her hand. In that single move, she looked so vulnerable. And now that he looked more closely, Derek could see her eyes were rimmed in red.

Maybe he wasn't being fair. He should give her a chance to explain. "What happened?" Striding to the cabinet above her kitchen sink, Derek snagged a lime-green mug. Flicking on Ashley's single-serve Keurig, he loaded it with a pod of dark roast grounds while waiting for the water to heat.

"I messed up Ben and Bella's invitations. Had to call the print shop, but I couldn't get ahold of anyone, so I drove there. But it's in San Luis, and traffic was worse than I thought it'd be."

The Keurig light came on, indicating the water was ready. Derek pushed the button, and the machine whirred to life before brown liquid began to stream into the mug. "Was anyone there?"

"Yes, and I waited while they printed up a new proof for me and a sample invitation that I could show Bella. When I got back to town, I ran it over to her place—"

Unbelievable. "So you actually were back in town, what? An hour or two ago?"

"Maybe an hour and a half?" Ashley set down her cup. "But Bella and I needed to work out a few more details about the invitations—who was going to pay for the oversight, when she'd get the redone invites, that kind of thing."

The intoxicating aroma of the coffee assaulted his senses, making him desperate for a swig. Derek yanked the mug out from under the Keurig, and liquid splashed over the edge.

He reached for the wet rag draped over the kitchen faucet and wiped up the spill. "And you just had to do all of this tonight?"

Ashley tapped her fingers along the edge of her mug, lips

pursed. "They need to mail their invites this week. I couldn't put it off."

"Really?" His laughter had an edge to it. "Twelve hours was going to make that much of a difference?"

For a moment, neither of them spoke. Ashley chewed her bottom lip, and he had to look away, to remember that whatever he felt for her, it was a chemical reaction. It didn't mean what he'd thought it meant.

It couldn't, or he'd be pulverized. Again.

"Okay, I admit it. Maybe I was scared."

At that, his gaze snapped back to her.

She folded her arms around her middle. "Maybe I allowed this thing with the invitations to be an excuse. To put off talking with you."

"Since when do I frighten you?"

"*You* don't, but all the questions, the unknowns—those do." Her shirt bunched beneath her fisted hands. "Derek, why did you kiss me in my office? Why do you want to explore things with me? What do you really feel for me?"

She was asking him this, after he'd ended his engagement for her? After he'd risked everything for the chance to be with her? "Are you serious? I thought this was what you wanted."

Her face hardened, and she scrubbed a hand over her mouth. "Maybe we should talk about this when we're both a bit more rested. Things will seem clearer in the morning."

Who needed sleep? Things were pretty clear right about now. Ashley Baker hadn't meant it when she'd claimed to love him. Love wasn't just words. It was action. And her actions spoke loud and clear about her priorities and where her heart really stood.

A least one thing *did* seem clear—if he really loved her, then he'd attached his heart to a woman who was going to keep stomping all over it. Dangling him on a fish hook. A fickle woman just like his mother, who had told her family how much she loved them.

But when push came to shove, she'd left them.

No thanks.

If this is what love did to people, then he'd be just fine with leaving it in the dust.

"I think we were just kidding ourselves, Ashley." He gestured between them. "This would never work."

With his coffee untouched and growing cold on the counter-top, Derek pivoted and headed for the door, letting it slam behind him.

CHAPTER 16

*I*t wasn't often that a woman came face-to-face with complete and utter failure.

But for Ashley, today was that day.

Steeling herself and swallowing hard, she lifted a hand to knock on Kyle's office door.

"Come in."

She pushed open the door to find her boss tucked over his morning cup of joe, two donuts from the Frosted Cake sitting on a plate next to his computer mouse.

"Good morning."

Kyle glanced up, lifting a bushy eyebrow in her direction. "Is it?"

Sighing, Ashley plopped into the chair opposite him. She wasn't going to pull one over on him, not with her bloodshot eyes that on other people might indicate a hangover. Well, she was hungover in one respect—she'd drunk a double shot of regret last night and chased it with a pint of heartache.

She shouldn't have gone to the print shop last night. Derek was completely right on that one.

But maybe, in the end, it was better to focus on helping Ben and Bella have their happily ever after than chase her own. After all, the man she loved couldn't even tell her why he wanted to be with her.

"I thought this was what you *wanted."* Like he didn't want it too. Or, at the very least, like he didn't know if he did.

Kyle cleared his throat, and Ashley was back in the present. "Sorry." She forced a thin smile. "I didn't sleep much last night." Or at all.

Her boss studied her, then pushed the plate across the desk. "Looks like you could use this more than me."

The apple fritter did look heavenly, and Ashley wouldn't mind the sugar infusion to steady her nerves. After all, she'd come here for a reason. "Thanks." Pinching a bit off the pastry, she stuck it in her mouth. The glaze melted on her tongue.

"Now, tell me why you're here at this ungodly hour."

She stole a napkin from the stack on his desk. "Eight o'clock is ungodly?"

"It is for you." Her boss fiddled with the end of his mustache. "Are you here to tell me what exactly happened with the Boivin-Campbell wedding?"

He'd been scouting an out-of-town venue with a couple yesterday when she'd learned the news, so Ashley hadn't had a chance to fill him in on the details yet—just told him that the wedding was canceled. He deserved the truth, especially because it would likely reflect poorly on him that his wedding coordinator had essentially broken up a bride and groom. But right now, her shattered heart couldn't take telling him.

What she'd actually come to say would negate all of that anyway.

"No." Ashley tugged at the paper napkin in her lap, which split neatly at the seams. "I wanted to let you know I don't want the business anymore." She grimaced as she glanced up. "Well, that's not exactly true. It's not that I don't want it as much as I can't handle it. You were right. I'm too busy. I … I just can't give it the priority that Cathy's legacy deserves."

"Hogwash." Kyle yanked the plate back to his side of the desk.

"I'm sorry, Kyle. I didn't mean to let you down." *To let everyone down.*

The festival committee.

Madison and Shannon, friends who deserved more from her.

Then, the last straw—Ben and Bella, her family. If Ashley couldn't be there for them, couldn't show them love, then what did it matter if she achieved her own dreams?

"This is the only way." Ashley reached for the plate again, stealing another bite of the fritter before Kyle tugged it out of her grasp. Eyeing him, she placed the sugar-laden treat in her mouth and swallowed.

There was no pleasure in being right.

Kyle frowned, then turned to the garbage and dumped the uneaten donuts off the plate and into the trash. "I don't care if you don't want the business." He opened his desk drawer and pulled out a folder. "I already signed it over to you."

"What?" Her stomach cramped as she reached for the folder, pulling it into her lap. "But we didn't work out the payment plan."

"Doesn't matter. I was prepared to give it to my niece without a fee. Why not someone I hold in even higher regard?"

Ashley's eyes stung as they pored over the papers in front of her—official documents naming her the owner of Whimsical Weddings & More. Her hands shook as she closed the folder and pushed it back across the desk. "I can't accept." He didn't know the whole truth about Derek and Claire's wedding. "I stole the groom."

A smirk tweaked the side of Kyle's mouth. "You don't live in a town with Carlotta Jenkins and not hear a little gossip now and again. But I don't believe for a second that you stole anyone. Mr. Campbell stopped by himself yesterday afternoon and cleared the whole situation up."

"He did?" *What did he say?* The words stuck to the roof of her mouth like the fritter had moments before.

"Yes, and so I don't blame you one bit. In fact, I applaud you for finally going after what you want. Now if they'd actually been in love, that might have been another story, but in this case, I believe all worked out as it should have."

He didn't know the half of it, and this didn't feel like the right time to tell him. Instead, Ashley focused on the papers in her lap. "I'm glad you don't think badly of me, but there's more to this decision than just the situation with Derek." Her finger slid lightly along the right edge of the folder. "I've failed a lot of people lately, just like you were afraid I would. And I've just realized that I can't choose my dreams over them."

Leaning back in his chair, Kyle folded his hands across his stomach. "That's not exactly what I'd hoped you'd learn in all of this."

"No?"

"I wanted you to learn that you can't be all things to all people."

"But what about *my* people?" Her bottom lip quivered. "I've let them down in some big ways."

"And if they're really your people, they'll forgive you for your failings, just like you forgive them when they fail you." Her boss tilted his head. "Think about this. How many of the things on your plate are actually all about being there for your people? Or are they more about feeling like if you don't volunteer for this or help with that, you aren't gonna be important to anyone? Because let me tell you something, little miss. That's not how love works. Do you love other people for what they do for you?"

"Of course not."

"And the same can be said about you. Your sense of self-worth can't come from what others think about you, because that's always changing."

She didn't think that. But she couldn't deny the extra burst of pleasure and relief she got when she did something for someone else—as if by doing so, she convinced herself they'd keep her around. "So where do we find it, then?"

Kyle took off his cowboy hat and scratched the top of his bald head. "You've gotta draw from somewhere deeper. Some find meaning in God, some just by looking within. All I know is that you have inherent value because you're a human being, and you're entitled to life, liberty, and the pursuit of happiness. So you should try leaning into that last one."

"But what if what I want isn't what others want?" She shoved the image of Derek away, because this ... this went deeper than that.

"If those others are really your people, they'll want you to be happy. Period." Twirling his hat, Kyle set it on his desk with a thump. "And if they're not, then who cares what they want? Those people aren't worth your time and attention anyway. Those people will scoop you dry until you're a hollowed-out well of a person with nothing left to give and no source to draw from." He paused. "Those are not the people you should be sacrificing for."

A tear leaked out from the corner of Ashley's eyes and dripped onto the cream-colored folder. Because even though it wasn't the first time she'd heard his words, this was the first time she'd heard the complete truth in them. She had striven her whole life to be what everyone else wanted and needed, but the people who really mattered had never asked her to do that. If she'd said no to any of them, they would have kept on loving her just as much as they always had.

As much as they were her people, she was theirs too.

And yeah, maybe she couldn't include Derek in that anymore. But with or without him, her life, her soul held meaning simply because she had been created with inherent value and purpose. And for her, that purpose included helping people.

But it didn't mean being a doormat.

She smiled, and this time, she didn't have to force it. "You're pretty wise, you know that?"

"You don't get to be my age without learning a few things." Kyle stared at her, a rare look of pride shining in his eyes. "And I've learned to trust my instincts. There's no one else that would be better suited to carry on my Cathy's legacy than you."

Ashley swallowed hard. "That means the world. Thank you."

He grunted. "Just calling it like I see it." Behind him on the wall, the clock ticked loudly, its hands rounding toward eight-thirty. A new workday was about to begin. "So what's it gonna be? Are you going to sacrifice all that you've worked for because you're afraid people won't love you if you don't make time for the things *they* want you to make time for? Or are you gonna start saying no to the things that don't matter and pursue the happiness coming to you?"

She closed her eyes for a brief second, imagined the possibilities, the future she held in her hands. Vaulting out of her chair, she circled the desk and hugged Kyle around the neck.

He patted her forearms with his large, rough hands. "Is that a yes?"

"Yes! It's most definitely a yes."

CHAPTER 17

"Sorry I couldn't be of more help." Alex Rosche rose from the Campbells' kitchen table and walked with Derek toward the front door.

Derek waved him off. "I appreciate you coming out on such short notice." He eyed Alex's dress slacks, button-up shirt, and tie. "And right after work too. On a Friday night."

"Anything for my second family." As the son of Millie, the Campbells' long-time housekeeper and cook, Alex had been like a little brother running around the vineyard when they were all young. But the annoying, scrawny kid had actually grown up to be wicked smart and helpful. "And I know things aren't what you'd hoped, but you did come up with some good ideas for recovery."

Derek had hoped that, as the city's financial analyst, Alex would be able to offer some extra insight into the vineyard's money troubles. He should have brought the guy in before now, but pride had gotten in the way. Not anymore.

Because now that he'd put his focus back where it should be —not on women and weddings, but on saving the vineyard—he would do anything it took. Unfortunately, the reality of their financial position had been worse than he'd thought.

If he didn't figure something out, by this time next year they'd have to sell off the vineyard, or at least part of it.

They reached the front door and Derek held out his hand to Alex. The guy shook it, then turned and headed toward his Corolla.

"What was Alex doing here?"

Derek shut the door and found Dad behind him leaning heavily on his cane. He'd had an infusion earlier today and looked ready to pass out.

"Nothing." His fingers itched to help Dad to the couch, but his father would chafe under that kind of attention. Instead, Derek headed back to the kitchen, where he gathered up the papers scattered across the tabletop.

"I just didn't know the two of you hung out that much. He's always been more Heather's friend than yours."

Apparently Dad had followed him.

The papers crinkled under Derek's hand as he stuffed them inside a folder. Derek sighed. Might as well tell Dad the truth. "I asked him to come over to do an assessment of our financials. We also chatted about some ideas I have for bringing in more revenue."

"Such as?"

He deposited the folder into his dad's available hand. "There are the smaller scale ideas, like renting out the cabins again. That used to bring in a nice tidy sum. I don't know why Heather suggested we stop that in the first place. We could also look into getting licensed to hold events on-site. There's some stupid city law right now, but I think they'd be a financial boon if we could get past that." Pacing, he ran a hand through his hair. "We also could sell off part of the land if we were really desperate. I know that's not ideal, but better to keep some of it if we can't keep it all. Oh, and we can approach some other vineyards to see if they want to partner with us."

Dad rapped his cane against the tile floor.

Derek froze, his gaze rounding on his father.

Shaking the folder, Dad's eyes narrowed. "Son, why didn't you run any of this by me before now?"

"You've had a lot going on." Much as he'd been chasing down his to-do list around the vineyard, house, and town, Derek couldn't have missed the very real toll dialysis had taken on his father. After a treatment, Dad slept for practically a full day—when he wasn't tied to the toilet, that was. "I didn't want to burden you."

"Burden me? This is *my* business."

"Yes, but …" He wanted to shake the stubbornness right out of his father. Biting back a groan, he beelined for the other side of the kitchen island where a pile of dirty dishes sat in the sink. Since he'd needed the kitchen after dinner and Millie had left early for a doctor's appointment, Derek had volunteered to clean up the mess Heather and Mia had left after making tacos for the whole family. No time like the present.

"But what?"

Dad wasn't going to like his answer. Derek flicked on the hot water, maneuvered around the dirty dishes to plug the sink, and squirted in some soap. "You're not the only one who wants to save it."

"Of course not." His dad eased onto the barstool at the island. "But ultimately, it's my responsibility."

"It's never just been *your* responsibility." Picking up the scrub brush, he attacked the first plate. "You're not the only one willing to do whatever it takes to save our home."

The kitchen grew silent except for splashing water and grinding bristles against the ceramic plates. Then, "What are we talking about here, son?"

But Derek couldn't tell him. It would break the man's pride. "Nothing." He dunked the plate into the soapy water, a bit of crusted-on refried beans clinging stubbornly to the stoneware.

"You weren't in love with Claire, were you?"

The plate slipped from Derek's hand and shattered on the floor.

Great. Just great.

Derek glanced up at Dad, prepared to see condemnation in his eyes—or disappointment, at the very least. But instead, something like sadness rested there.

Sighing, he glanced down at the mess he'd created. "No, I wasn't. I respected her and she respected me, but ..." He shrugged.

"I never asked that of you, son."

"You didn't have to. Like I said. Whatever it takes." Squatting, he opened the cabinet under the sink and pulled out the hand broom and dustpan. Then he turned and swept up the largest pieces of the plate he'd broken.

"I should never have let you do so much after your mother left."

Derek peeked up.

Dad's head was in his hands. "I thought it would help you, to give you a purpose, but I didn't realize I'd actually given the impression that everything was on your shoulders."

"What do you mean?" Frowning, Derek returned to the cleanup. He'd need to grab a vacuum, but that could wait. This conversation was too important to be interrupted. "You knew I was doing all of that?"

"Of course I knew. You were only ten years old. I would never have put that weight on you." His dad's voice rang with conviction. Then he barked out a staccato laugh. "I paid Jorge extra to give you some things to do, watch out for you, and redo anything you didn't get right."

"I had no idea." Derek scooped the last visible bits of the broken plate into the dustpan and tossed them into the trash. "You were so torn up about Mom. I thought I was helping you."

The bitterness of the truth settled in his mouth. Much as he'd tried to help, he'd really only been a nuisance to poor Jorge. The man was a saint to have put up with him back then.

He reached for the pan Heather had used to cook the taco meat, and the scent of the leftover spicy seasonings inflamed his nose.

"Yes, I was torn up about your mother, but never so much that I forgot about you." A pause. "And you helped more than you know. You and your sisters saved me from my grief. You were my gift in the darkness."

The back of his eyes burned, and Derek scrubbed the pan in front of him harder. "I'm glad to have that all cleared up, but what about the here and now? What do we do about the vineyard?"

Dad sighed. "I've been going over it every which way, and I've approached some other vineyards for partnerships, but so far nothing has worked out."

Wait, what? "Why didn't you say anything to me about that?" He let his hands rest in the soapy water as he directed his gaze once more at Dad.

"I didn't want to burden my children with my mistakes. I got us into this mess with all of those medical bills. I thought I needed to dig us out of the hole I'd made. Sounds like we both suffer from the same stubborn affliction, huh?"

Derek smirked. "Guess so."

"Maybe we need to work together to make this thing a success."

He finished up the last of the dishes, then pulled the plug on the drain. "I like the sound of that." Drying his hands on a towel, he slipped around the island and took the seat next to Dad. "I know the ideas I've come up with aren't much, but they're something."

"I'm intrigued by the events idea. What would it take to get licensed?"

"I'm not positive. There's some obscure law from the eighties about not allowing events to take place at wineries because they wanted to preserve the land for agricultural use. But I'm guessing we can petition the city council to revoke or revisit that law."

Dad reached for the cookie jar next to him and pulled out an Oreo. "And if it's really as easy as all that, maybe you can work with Ashley to book some weddings here in the near future."

Aw, man.

When he'd told Dad about breaking things off with Claire, he'd failed to mention Ashley. Mostly because by then, *that* had been a failure too. And now, three days after things had ended so terribly, he'd finally gone almost a full hour without thinking of her.

But how easy it was for the mere mention of her to crash against his chest, making it difficult to breathe.

"Yeah, sure." Derek crammed his hand into the jar and grabbed three cookies for himself.

"Something you need to talk about?" His dad scrutinized Derek's dessert.

Ignoring him, Derek twisted open a cookie, then dropped it as a memory assailed him.

Ashley dunked her Oreo into her cup and took a bite. "Mmm. Milk makes Oreos taste so much better."

Derek rolled his eyes. "That's no way to eat an Oreo. You've got to lick off all the cream first and eat the chocolate pieces separately."

Laughing, she reached for another. "I'll try it your way, then."

"Just like that?"

"Why not?" She split the cookie and handed him half. "What's life without a little adventure?"

"Eating cookies is not an adventure."

"But sharing them with friends is."

He shoved the two pieces of Oreo aside, then turned toward his dad. "How did you get over Mom?"

If his dad was surprised by the question, he didn't show it. Just chewed his cookie thoughtfully and wiped his fingers with a napkin, then swigged from a water bottle. "I'm not sure you ever get over someone you love. They become part of you. So does the pain."

Scrubbing a hand across his face, Derek groaned. "That's what I'm afraid of."

"But." His dad scooted another cookie across the counter toward Derek. "That pain eventually lessens with time. And the lessons you learned get sharper."

"See, the lesson I figured you'd have learned is to not trust women again. And yet you and Nancy seem happy enough."

"We're very happy. I'd have been a fool if I let one woman's unfaithfulness and instability make up my mind about the whole gender. Some people can let you down, but you don't throw the baby out with the bathwater. Because people are also what makes life beautiful." He placed his hand on Derek's shoulder. "Think about this. Why is the vineyard worth saving?"

"It's our legacy."

"You going to care about a legacy after you're gone?"

Derek shrugged.

"So try again. Why is the vineyard worth saving?"

"Because it means the world to you. To Heather. To Christina. It represents …" Oh man, he sounded like a total sap. "Family. History. Love."

Whew. There went that burning at the back of his eyes again.

"Exactly. Your heart's in the right place, Derek. Everything you've done, you've done for love. You just didn't want to call it that because you were afraid of what it meant. But there's no shame in love. Love is the only thing worth living for." A pause. "What happened with Ashley, son?"

Derek fiddled with the cookie Dad had shoved his way, his father's words stinging something deep inside. "She doesn't love me. I was a fool to think she might."

Then Dad laughed.

Seriously?

Derek narrowed his eyes. "What's so funny?"

"If you believe that she doesn't love you, you really are a fool." A squeeze to his shoulder. "That girl has had eyes for you since she was a teenager."

Shaking his head, Derek recounted their last conversation. "She had the gall to ask me what I felt for her. As if it weren't completely obvious." The way he'd looked at her, the emotion in that kiss, not to mention ending his wedding … all of it pointed to one clear conclusion.

"You have a lot to learn about women."

That was sure the truth.

Dad tapped a cookie against the counter. "Even if you think your actions were obvious, as you say, women sometimes need those words of reassurance anyway. Have you ever actually told her you love her?"

And he was an idiot. "No."

"That's probably a good place to start."

Hope had the nerve to break through the wall he'd built around his heart. "Do you think that will work?" Whirling toward the table, he snatched his keys. "I'll go right now."

"Sit down, son. It's late. Besides, you need to really think about what you're going to say and how you're going to say it." Biting into a cookie, Dad chewed and swallowed. "Sounds to me like you need to go big or go home. Make a splash."

A splash. Right.

Derek strode toward the fridge, pulled out a gallon of milk, poured himself a drink, and came back to the counter with it. For a moment, he stared at the cup.

Then, he grabbed an Oreo and tossed it all the way into his milk. A bit of the liquid sloshed over the side before Derek fished out the cookie and took a bite.

"Milk makes Oreos taste so much better."

Yeah. Actually, it really did.

CHAPTER 18

*D*ays like today were normally Ashley's favorite.

But even being surrounded by family and the town she loved, something was missing.

Not something. Someone.

The smell of grilling hamburgers and hot dogs filled the air of the community park tucked away in a residential area on the wooded side of town. Across the grassy expanse, townspeople huddled together, eating and drinking on blankets and in folding chairs they'd brought for the annual Memorial Day weekend picnic put on by the Sons of the American Legion and the Legion Auxiliary.

Some kids tossed a ball around on the baseball field in the distance, and members of Walker Beach High's band—directed by Ashley's uncle Mark West—played a rousing rendition of "God Bless America" from the small stage assembled near the ramadas.

Yet despite all the people, the Campbell family was nowhere to be seen. Maybe that was not surprising, since today should have been Derek's wedding. Could be they were avoiding the gossips.

Ashley shook free of the melancholy that inevitably came when she thought about him. No. Not today. Not when the sun was shining and her friends and family were all gathered, not when summer and all the good things were just on the horizon, not when she was free to follow her dreams because of this great nation and all the men and women who had died defending it. *That's* what today was really about.

Her time spent cleaning up the veterans' cemetery with her family this morning had been a sober reminder of all the good in her life thanks to the sacrifice of those they honored this Memorial Day. And Ashley was going to enjoy every moment, even when she felt like doing otherwise.

She thanked the volunteer who placed a burger on her plate, then made her way down the food line toward the assortment of potato salads, pasta salads, fruit salads, green salads, and baked beans. After taking a small sampling of each, Ashley took a bag of chips and a chocolate chip cookie before making her way toward one of the many Baker family blankets spread near the front of the crowd.

"Ashley Baker! Just the woman I was hoping to see."

Turning toward the jovial voice, she found Bud Travis waving her down as he huffed toward her.

"How are you, Bud?" Ashley offered her warmest smile as she shifted the plate in her hands.

Bud's nearly bald head glistened under the noon-time sun. "I'm good. Real good, actually. Decided to run for mayor this fall."

"Wow, that's great." The town could certainly use a mayor who actually cared about its people—not just his power. And thus far, Mayor Walsh was running uncontested. "What made you decide to do that?"

"Velma." The whiskers from Bud's long white beard and mustache couldn't disguise the man's grin. "She made little comments here and there in that quiet way of hers about things we could do to improve the town. It finally got through my thick skull that maybe I should do something other than stew about them."

"I'm happy for you." She leaned in. "And you've already got my vote."

"Wonderful! But I'm hoping you can do more for me than that."

"Oh?" As it usually did, word had spread quickly about her taking over Kyle's business. "I'm happy to throw you a victory party when the time comes." She winked.

The skin around his tan face wrinkled even more with his laugh. "That would be good too, but I was more thinking along the lines of you being my campaign manager. Don't know anyone more organized and better with people than you."

"Me?" Sure, she'd grown up in this town and knew everyone, but politics were way down there on her list of interests, right next to dieting and reading. "Um, I'm honored."

Bud studied her, lips moving to the side. "Now, don't feel like you need to answer right away. I can give you some time to examine your schedule."

"No, that's not necessary." She should do it, for the good of the town, right?

Her eyes swept the park, filled with all—almost all—of the people she loved best. There were Evan and Madison, and Shannon and Bella and Ben, and Ms. Josephine and Aunt Jules and Mom and Dad. Even Carlotta Jenkins, who sat like a queen in a chair surrounded by her hive of honeybees, brought something to the town.

You can't be all things to all people. Kyle's voice was in her head.

Bud's eyes twinkled. "I hope that smile means you're considering saying yes."

"Actually, I'm going to have to say no. I would love to help you out, but my plate is pretty full right now." She looked down. "And I don't just mean the one in my hand."

He chuckled.

Here went nothing. "I also have to admit that I don't think I'd have the level of passion for the project that I should." She cringed as the words rushed out. What would he say to her honesty?

Nodding, he stroked his beard. "I'm disappointed, but I understand."

Incredible. Bud genuinely wasn't mad at her. Kyle had been right—those who loved her would keep loving her, no matter what she did or didn't do for them.

"Know anyone who might be available and good at the job?"

Her mind immediately latched on to the perfect answer. "Kyle Mahaney. He's the kind of guy who won't be able to sit still in retirement for long."

"I know the feeling." Bud scratched behind his ear. "I'll give him a call next week and see what he thinks. Thank you for the suggestion. I'd better let you go eat now."

"Of course." She waved goodbye and turned to look for an opening on her family's blanket, which was sheltered by the trees ringing the large grassy area that took up most of the park.

Aunt Jules waved Ashley over, patting the spot next to her. "Well, if it isn't the newest Baker family business owner."

Sitting between Jules and Bella, Ashley settled her plate on the soft blue blanket. "Thanks for making room for me."

"There's always a place with us." Jules nudged Ashley's shoulder. "We're all very proud of you."

Ashley peeked at Bella, who watched her. Blood rushed to her cheeks. She hadn't seen her friend since dropping off her and Ben's new—and correctly printed—invites a few days ago. They'd both been in a rush to get out the door, so Ashley hadn't been able to tell if the couple was still upset about her screwup.

She shrugged. "Kyle ended up giving me the business, which

was very kind of him." Picking up her fork, she poked at some of the food on her plate. "It was a gift, but I'm determined to do my best with it."

"Any bride will be lucky to have you in her corner." Bella bit her lip.

Ashley's chest constricted.

Ben took a swig of Coke from his can. "We really appreciate all you've done for us, sis."

"Agreed." Bella paused. "And I shouldn't have freaked out like I did. Will you forgive me?"

Did she even have to ask? "If you'll forgive me for messing up your invitations."

"Nothing to forgive. It was an honest mistake."

They hugged, and Ashley finally tucked into her food. That first bite of her charcoal-grilled burger was heavenly. Ms. Josephine's husband, Arnie, had outdone himself this time.

Behind her, the band ended their compilation of all the armed forces' theme songs with a squeak, and the crowd clapped.

Ashley lifted her burger for another bite.

"Excuse me."

Her eyes widened at the voice coming over the microphone, and the burger in her hands tumbled to her plate.

Derek?

Ashley twisted to see him up on the stage, the microphone tucked under his arm as he led the crowd in clapping. What was he doing? He hated being in the spotlight. Had nearly failed his public speaking final in college—or so he'd told her.

What would possess him to be up there now?

"Hi, everyone. Thanks for coming out today. Not that I had anything to do with the whole thing, but ... uh, yeah."

All around her, townspeople murmured.

He ran a hand through his hair and pulled the mic back to

his mouth. "I confess that I may have slipped Mark West a twenty to commandeer the stage for a moment."

"I'm donating it to the Legion, don't you worry, Arnie!" Uncle Mark called from his spot to the right of the stage.

Arnie Radcliffe banged his tongs against the grill. "You'd better be!"

A laugh rippled through the crowd.

But Ashley couldn't laugh, couldn't do anything but swallow hard at the sight of the man who had broken her heart again. She barely felt the hand Bella placed on her knee.

Derek waited for the laughter to die down. "I know you're all wondering what I'm doing up here, but much as I like you guys, this really has nothing to do with any of you." A pause. "Well, that's not true. It has to do with exactly one of you."

He stepped to the very edge of the stage. Then his eyes found Ashley's, and she froze.

Despite the size of the park and the number of people in it, the only sound Ashley heard was the whoosh of pounding blood in her ears and the drumming of her heart.

"Most of you know that I was supposed to be getting married today. I'm sure there are a lot of rumors floating around about why my fiancée and I ended things."

Another rustling of whispers.

"But let me tell you the absolute truth of the matter so there's no doubt in anyone's mind. I never loved Claire and she never loved me. We had our reasons for getting married, and when those things didn't work out, we ended it amicably." Even from the distance between them, Ashley could see the sweat shining off his forehead. "I'm telling you this not because I care what any of you think of me but because I don't want you saying one bad thing about the woman that I *do* love."

Oh, goodness.

Then he left that stage with the cordless mic in hand and walked toward the Bakers' blanket.

Bella's hand felt like a vise grip on Ashley's knee.

When he'd finally made his way to Ashley, Derek squatted in front of her. "You asked me what I felt for you, and I was afraid to tell you the truth. Afraid of your rejection. Afraid that if I put my heart out there, you'd leave me like ... others have done."

Sweet man.

She couldn't help it. Ashley lifted her hand to stroke his cheek.

His voice lowered to a whisper that boomed over the mic. "But here's the truth. Ashley Baker, I love you. Only you."

"I love you too."

Then the mic plopped onto the grass and Derek was kissing her in front of the whole town.

The whole town—who, she realized, was cheering.

Ashley laughed and buried her face in Derek's shoulder. "I can't believe you just did that."

"Was that enough of a splash?"

"A splash?" She pulled back to look at him.

"Never mind." He swooped in to kiss her again. "Want to get out of here? Or did you promise your family you'd stay?"

The question in his eyes was so vulnerable, as if he truly wondered if she'd choose her family over him again. Well, she'd just clear that one right up once and for all.

"I was going to stay, but I'm sure they'll understand." Ashley kissed his cheek. "And if they don't, that's on them. Because right now, there's nowhere else I'd rather be than with you."

CHAPTER 19

*A*nother hard week of satisfying work in her rearview mirror. Another Friday night date with the man she loved in the headlights ahead. The stars popped out one by one in the sky, Ashley bearing witness to it all as she drove down the remote dirt road toward the Campbells' vineyard.

Her fingers drummed on the steering wheel. "So everything is all set for a week from Sunday, then?"

"I think so." Shannon's voice filtered through the car's speakers. "I'm still nervous I've forgotten something."

"I wouldn't have put you in charge of the reunion if I'd thought you couldn't handle it." Ashley had done most of the legwork before handing it over to her eager-to-help cousin a couple of weeks ago, anyway. "And I'll be there for most of it supporting you. I asked Kyle to handle anything with the business so I can be fully committed to the reunion and Ben and Bella's wedding activities."

The full moon split the sky. Amazing how much brighter everything was out here where there weren't any lights. Her tires bit and flicked rocks as they rotated down the road.

"I still can't believe so many people are coming, though the wedding seems to be the main draw." Shannon's golden retriever, Lucky, barked in the background. "Did I tell you Quinn's bringing a guy with her? They're arriving next Saturday."

"Really?" Shannon's older sister and Tyler's twin lived in New York City as some sort of hotshot marketing executive, and she hadn't been home for several years—not even for her brother's wedding last fall. "I'll bet your mom is thrilled."

"Yeah, someone to give us actual insight into my sister's life. You know, since Quinn doesn't like telling us more than she's uber successful and can get any guy she wants."

Quinn was the only subject that made Shannon sarcastic. It must be exhausting living in her older sister's shadow.

Ashley sighted the vineyard lights. Normally she'd head directly to Derek's cabin, but he'd asked her to come to the main house tonight—and not until eight-thirty, a bit later than they usually met. "Well, hey, I'm almost to Derek's. Anything else you're feeling unsure about?"

Shannon heaved a sigh. "Not about the reunion, no."

"Something else?" Nearly three weeks of learning how to run a business and balancing a new relationship hadn't left much time for her and Shannon to connect outside of their reunion planning meetings.

"I've made a decision. Just told my parents last night."

"About what?" Pulling up to the house, Ashley put the car in park.

A stream of heavy breath hit the phone, crackling over the sound waves. "I've decided to adopt Noah Robinson."

"What?"

"I know. It's a huge decision, but his grandma's been moved to a memory care facility. Social services has tried locating his mother and other family members and they just can't find anyone. Mary's nearest neighbor up the road is still keeping Noah, but she's moving away in a few months." Shannon's voice trembled. "Ash, he's the sweetest kid, and I just can't sit by and let him go into the system. He'd probably have to leave Walker Beach, be far away from the one family member he has."

"Oh, Shan. You're the most generous person I know." Ashley bit her lip. "Are you sure about this? You'll be a single mom. That's hard work."

"It's much harder to think that I could have done something and didn't."

"What did your parents say?"

"They're still kind of hesitant, I think. But I'm hoping they come around." Shannon grew quiet. "What do *you* think?"

The front door of Derek's house opened and Heather stepped out. She waved when she saw Ashley sitting in the car.

Ashley returned the wave. "I think you'll be a great mom, and I'm happy to help you any way I can."

"Thank you, cuz. That means the world."

After they said goodbye, Ashley blew out a breath. Wow. The thought of being a single mom—that was tough. But Heather Campbell rocked at it, as did a few others Ashley knew. Shannon would be great.

Speaking of Heather, she was still standing on the front porch.

Ashley shut the car off and climbed out. "Hey, girl."

"Hey, yourself. Derek asked me to tell you to head to his cabin after all. But he wants you to walk. Oh, and you can leave your purse with me."

Smiling, Ashley lifted a brow. "Mysterious."

Derek's sister strode forward, gently took the purse Ashley held out, and pointed toward the vineyard. "Go that way."

Ah. Derek wanted to meet in their special spot. They'd been there several times since they'd finally stopped beating around the bush and declared their love for each other. "Thanks, Heather."

Heather winked and disappeared back into the house.

Ashley started her trek through the vineyard. The moon's light made the young grape clusters visible. Sooner than she could imagine, they'd be maturing into full-grown fruit ready for harvest.

As she approached the clearing in the middle of the vines, Ashley curved around a bend and pulled up short. Her hand flew to her mouth as her heart thudded against her ribs.

Luminaries lined the path in front of her.

As if on air, Ashley walked between the first pair, eyes peeled for anything else that didn't belong.

And there, fluttering on the breeze, was a note clipped to a clothesline that had been tied to stakes in the ground—a line that traveled into the distance, beyond where Ashley could see. Next to the note hung a small flashlight no bigger than Ashley's hand, which trembled as she reached for it. After clicking the light on, she plucked the note from the string.

Derek's neat, uniform handwriting filled the page.

I remember the first time we were on the same team.

It was Ben's thirteenth birthday party, and he invited me to go bowling with your family. You and I got paired together, and I remember groaning because I was sure I'd lose with a little girl on my side. But you showed us all.

I'll never forget your victory dance when you scored the winning shot. Even at the age of ten, you were teaching me not to underestimate you—and also, that I loved being on your team.

She folded the note and held it against her heart. Oh, this man.

Moving down the lane, she came across another note. And

another. And another. Each one spoke of precious memories of their early friendship.

Her chest expanded at the implications of what was happening. Was this real?

She picked up the fifth note.

I remember the first time I almost got up the courage to kiss you. It was about a year after we started hanging out without Ben around. We'd just gone running down the path near the lodge, and of course, you'd challenged me to a race. And yeah, you beat me, but we won't talk about that.

I'd fallen for you months before, but had been content to just get to know you better as someone other than my best friend's little sister. Well, you started doing that same victory dance you did at the bowling alley, swinging your hips around, smiling up a storm, and man, I nearly snagged you around the waist and laid one on you right then and there. Figured that would shut you up and give me something to gloat about.

But some dumb tourists came tearing up the hiking path and ruined the moment. I knew there was a reason I hated tourists.

Hysterical giggles bubbled from her throat.

She looked up, then swallowed hard. Nearly there.

Ashley made her way to the edge of the clearing, gasping at the gorgeous setup in front of her. Tall poles had been placed around the circle and used to mount twinkle lights that criss-crossed overhead. Underneath sat a soft-looking nest of blankets and pillows alongside an ice bucket with a bottle of wine sticking out.

She glanced around the clearing but didn't see Derek anywhere. Huh.

Ashley reached for one last note clipped to the end of the clothesline.

Do you remember that time I asked you to be my wife?
No?
Turn around, Ash. Our future awaits.

Spinning, Ashley faced the clearing once more—and nearly choked on a gasp.

There Derek kneeled, a red velvet box in his hand. "I see you found my notes."

She had them all clutched in her left hand. "They're beautiful."

"They're true. Every last memory. Every sentiment." He gazed up at her, the lights from above illuminated in his eyes. "Ashley, I know we haven't been together officially for all that long, but I've loved you for years and I'm tired of waiting. You are everything I want in a partner."

Tears strolled down her cheeks.

Derek continued. "I can't imagine living my life without you beside me, helping me to be a better man, encouraging me to strive for more than the status quo. You turned my world upside down, but I've realized that upside down is exactly where I want to be." He popped open the ring box, revealing a one-carat, princess-cut solitaire on a white gold band. "So, Ashley Baker, will you marry me?"

Sinking to her knees on the cool dirt, she nodded. "Of course I'll marry you, Derek. You're all I've waited for. And more."

Taking her trembling hand in his, he slid the ring onto her fourth finger. It settled in as if it had belonged to her for years instead of seconds. "It's perfect."

Derek hooked his hands around her waist, drawing her closer. "You're perfect."

"No." She placed her hand on his chest, admiring the shimmers of the diamond. *"We're* perfect. Together."

"I won't argue with that." And dipping his head, he caught her lips with his own, proving the truth in her statement over and over and over again.

EPILOGUE

*E*very day with Ashley was an adventure.

But especially today.

Derek grabbed a spot in the boat club's parking lot. Ashley had asked him to meet at her cousin Nate's boat. How she'd found time to plan a surprise date the day before her family's big reunion, Derek didn't have a clue. But he was grateful for any extra time he could get with her. Since asking her to be his wife eight days ago, he'd barely seen the woman.

Hopping out of his Jeep, Derek headed toward the pier. Another cloudless blue sky greeted him and the wind off the sea whistled a hello. Someone yelled "Fore!" from the golf course that abutted the ocean to the north, and Derek maneuvered around a group of people gathered at the entrance to the small marina. Really, it was just a dock with fifteen or so slips, but the boats parked there ranged in size from small motorboats to yachts.

The pier was crowded today, not surprising for a Saturday in June, but he found Ashley with no problem about five slips down. She was standing near a sleek black-and-white motor yacht chatting with her cousin Spencer.

When she saw him approach, she grinned. "Hey!" Her tan had deepened with the days of summer, her hair turned even lighter. But the most beautiful thing about her was the weight that no longer dragged her shoulders down. Smiles had always come frequently for Ashley, but the one she zinged at him today was carefree and filled with joy.

He loved seeing her this way. He loved her.

"Hey, yourself." Derek caught her around the waist and kissed her. How quickly that had become second nature—and he was the lucky guy who would get to kiss her every day for the rest of his life.

A throat cleared and Derek looked up. Oh yeah. Spencer. One hand still tucked around Ashley, he reached out the other. "Hey, man. Shouldn't you be preparing for a sermon or something?" He grinned at his future cousin-in-law, who looked a lot more like a football linebacker than a pastor.

Spencer chuckled as he shook Derek's hand. "Got that done earlier this week, man. Today I get the privilege of motoring you guys around."

"You know how to drive that thing?"

Ashley tapped Derek's chest. "Of course he does. It's his brother's boat. And their dad made sure all of his kids—as well as us cousins—learned how to drive a boat too."

His eyebrows lifted. "Really? What other secret talents are you hiding from your fiancé?"

"Guess you'll have to discover them as we grow old and gray together." Ashley reclaimed her spot in his full embrace, and he couldn't help but steal another kiss. Or two.

Fine, three.

Yeah, he could definitely get used to this.

His ears filled with Spencer's laugh again. Derek groaned and dragged his mouth away, looking askance at the pastor. "Sorry not sorry, dude. You had to know what you were signing up for when you agreed to tag along."

"Oh, I knew exactly what I was signing up for." The man's blue eyes twinkled like he was Saint Nick. Then he turned and climbed onto the boat.

Derek returned his attention to the future Mrs. Campbell. "So where are we off to today?"

"That's for me to know and you to find out. But I promise it'll be memorable."

"With you, it always is."

He helped her onto the boat, which featured a pilothouse with large swing-bi-fold doors, an L-shaped settee, an inlaid table, and a two-person love seat. The transom featured fixed seating for enjoying the ride outdoors, which is where Ashley parked them both.

With Spencer shut away inside, the boat rumbled to life and pulled away from the marina. Salt spray skimmed Derek's cheeks as he held Ashley against his chest and enjoyed the sun on his face. Out here, the troubles with the vineyard—which were still a struggle, though he and Dad had made some headway on their goals—seemed far away.

His fingers fiddled with Ashley's white T-shirt, which fell off her shoulder, revealing the strap of her red bathing suit underneath. If he knew her, she'd be in the water as soon as Spencer found a good place to anchor for a bit.

They stayed like that for a long while, her breathing so steady and her so still, she must have fallen asleep.

At last, the boat came to a stop, and Derek peeked over the side. Land was just a tiny blip on the horizon. Out here in the middle of the ocean, it was just him, Ashley, and the waves.

Well, and Spencer, but he could forgive the man his intrusion since he'd given up his Saturday to chauffeur them around.

Ashley stirred in his arms. Poor woman was exhausted, and no wonder, with all the prep she'd been doing for Ben and Bella's wedding.

Derek leaned forward, feathering a kiss against her forehead.

"Rise and shine, beautiful." He hated to wake her, but she probably had their whole day planned and would be upset if she missed it.

She arched her back slightly, turning in his arms and tucking hers around his torso. "Hmm." Her sweet murmur flooded him with warmth. Soon—though not soon enough—he would get to wake up next to this woman every day.

Man, he was way luckier than he deserved.

Spencer opened the door to the pilothouse, stretching his bulky arms over his head. "She asleep?"

"Yeah."

They chatted for a bit about life and the upcoming reunion, and eventually their discussion roused Ashley. She sat up straight. "Derek Campbell, did you let me fall asleep?"

"You looked so peaceful."

"What time is it?" She glanced at the clock above the pilothouse. "Yikes. We're running late."

"Late for what? Our date with the fish?" Derek poked her in the ribs.

Spencer leaned against the boat rail, a knowing smile on his face.

Shaking free of Derek's hold, Ashley stood, her cheeks rosy as she leaned down and pressed her lips to his. "I'm going to the restroom to freshen up, and when I get back, you'd better be ready."

"To do what?"

"You'll see." And then in a flash, she disappeared down the stairs next to the cockpit.

His attention fixed on Spencer, Derek pointed in the direction she'd gone. "You know what that's about?"

Ashley's cousin just grinned and pulled a water bottle from the cooler hidden inside the bench seat next to Derek. "You don't really think I'm going to give away her secrets, do you?" He tossed the bottle to Derek, who caught it with one hand.

The sudden chill tingled his fingertips. "Guess not." He took a swig from the bottle and shot the breeze with Spencer for what seemed like an hour. What was Ashley doing down there? He thought she had her bathing suit on already, but maybe not. He'd worn his blue swim trunks and a white T-shirt, so he was all ready to go in the water once she finished up.

Finally, the door to the cabin below creaked open and her blonde head emerged. She climbed the stairs and Derek's jaw dropped at the sight of her standing in the doorway to the pilot-house wearing a long white dress that sparkled in the sunlight. It dipped just low enough in the front to make his mouth go dry despite all the water he'd just drunk. Her hair flowed around her shoulders, and a wreath of yellow flowers sat on her head. The ring he'd bought her winked from her fourth finger.

"Wow." Derek set his water bottle aside. "You look gorgeous."

A shy smile slid across her lips. "Gorgeous enough to get married?"

They hadn't even set a wedding date. Why was she showing him her wedding dress now? "What do you mean?"

She stepped forward and held out her hand. "I mean, do you want to get married? Today? Right now?"

"Seriously?" But the look on her face was anything but joking. "But don't you want all of our friends and family with us? The church? The flowers? The whole shebang?"

"No, Derek." She placed her hand against his chest. "I just want you. Besides, you never wanted a big wedding, and we'll have a reception in the winter, after the harvest is over. But I don't want to go another day without being Mrs. Derek Campbell."

His insides vibrated. "Are you sure?"

"Never been more sure of anything in my life."

"But don't we need a few things to get married?"

"You mean like the wedding license I dragged you to City Hall for last week?"

One of the only times he'd seen her last week, and he'd wondered at the hurry. But she'd assured him they might as well get it taken care of since it was the only thing on the future wedding checklist she could handle doing right then and there. "You sure fooled me."

She bounced on the balls of her feet, which were adorably bare despite the soft, fancy dress. "And we just so happen to have a pastor with us too. Imagine that."

Derek shook his head. "You thought of everything."

"So is that a yes?"

He whooped, taking her in his arms and twirling her around before setting her back down and kissing her senseless. "You better believe it."

"Good, because our witnesses are here."

At that moment, a small motorboat putted toward them, and Derek recognized the helmsman. "Evan? And is that Madison?"

"Yes." Ashley hesitated. "I know Ben and Bella would have loved to be here, but they're so busy getting ready for their own wedding next weekend. And Shannon is handling the reunion …"

Derek took her hand in his and kissed her fingertips. "Evan and Madison are perfect. I'm sure our families will understand, especially if we have a reception later."

"You think so? That's the only thing I'm not sure about."

"Ash, they love you. And if this is what you want—what will make you happy—then they'll be happy for you. For us."

She smiled up at him, her grin dazzling in the sunlight. "It is what I want."

"Good. Me too." He tipped her chin and kissed her.

"Hey, aren't you supposed to wait for a pronouncement or something?" Evan parked the boat off the back and he and Madison climbed aboard the motor yacht. The women hugged and Evan slapped Derek on the back. "Congrats, man."

"I just found out."

His friend grinned. "I know. Mad and I have been avoiding you all week so we didn't spoil the surprise. You have no idea how hard it was."

Derek punched Evan in the shoulder. "Just glad you're here."

Spencer stepped toward them, and with the sky and waves as their witnesses, he spoke the words Derek had only dreamed of hearing as Ashley's groom. Before Derek knew it, he was reciting his vows, and then Ashley was slipping a simple white gold band on his left hand.

"It's my great honor to pronounce you man and wife," the pastor said. "Derek, go ahead and kiss your bride."

Derek's chest swelled. His bride. How far they'd come, and how far they'd go.

But as for the going, they'd do it together.

With all the care he could manage, Derek took his beloved's face in his hands and melded her lips with his own. She tasted of sun and sea and the one thing he'd feared never to find.

A forever kind of love.

CONNECT WITH LINDSAY

Thanks so much for joining Ashley and Derek on their journey! I hope you loved them as much as I do. If so, would you mind doing me a favor and leaving a review on Goodreads, Bookbub, or your favorite retail site?

I'd love to connect with you. Sign up for my newsletter at www.lindsayharrel.com/subscribe and I'll send you a FREE story as a thank you!

Can't get enough of Walker Beach? You can read Shannon's story in the next book, *All You Need Is Love.* Turn the page for a sneak peek…

ALL YOU NEED IS LOVE SNEAK PEEK

Normally, life in the slow lane suited Shannon Baker just fine.

But three to six months to become a foster mom—to become Noah's mom?

That was an eternity.

The water lapped at her bare feet as she walked the wet shoreline, flip-flops dangling from her fingers. At eleven o'clock, the beach was already crowded with locals and tourists alike, but Shannon only had attention for the boy she hoped one day to adopt.

Several feet ahead, Noah Robinson tossed a football to Lucky and laughed as the golden retriever took off into the fringes of the California surf. Shannon closed her eyes for a moment, relishing the five-year-old's giggles pealing across the same breeze that lifted Shannon's hair off her shoulders.

Noah's joy, the late-June sun on Shannon's face, the crisp scent of coconut sunscreen and brine—it all soothed the parts of her soul left ruffled by the call she'd received from the adoption agency yesterday after work. The one that had stated she'd have to wait much longer than she'd hoped to bring Noah into her home.

Which meant he faced even more uncertainty. And his short life had already been filled with so much.

When combined with the thought that tonight she'd have to face her sister Quinn for the first time in forever—*thank you, Baker family reunion*—it was almost enough for Shannon to bury herself in a heap of blankets and stay curled up in bed all day watching Hallmark Christmas movies in the middle of summer.

But here she was, fighting the urge to turn inward. Fighting to keep the peace in her own heart. Fighting for Noah's sake.

The blond-haired boy raced after Lucky toward the north end of the beach, where rocks curved into a magnificent cove that divided the beach from a six-acre community park on the other side.

"Noah!" Shannon cupped her hands around her mouth. "Don't go too far."

"Okay!" But as soon as he reached the rocks, he disappeared from sight.

There wasn't anywhere for him to go past the rocky cove, and he could swim, but that didn't stop Shannon from chasing after him, her heart banging against her ribs until she caught sight of the boy hugging Lucky at the edge of the water. For the first time since she'd picked him up from his current foster home this morning, he'd stopped moving, staring out across the ocean.

He'd grown so much in the two years since she'd met him. A recent spurt had left his bathing suit two inches higher than his knee, but in this moment, he was the same three year old she'd had to comfort when his grandma Mary had dropped him off in Shannon's preschool classroom for the first time.

The faraway gaze in his precious blue eyes, the way he bit his bottom lip so it didn't tremble, his arms wrapped tight around Lucky's neck—they all socked Shannon in the gut, a reminder that he was lost. No matter how brave and confident and friendly he'd grown since that first day of school, a boy simply didn't get over his mother leaving him behind to chase other dreams.

And with his former-neighbor-turned-foster-mom moving out of state by the end of the summer, he needed someone he could count on. She wanted to be that person.

Shannon dropped her shoes on the ground, squatted beside Noah, and placed her hand on his back. "You okay, bud?"

He glanced at her, his freckled nose scrunched. "Miss Florence is taking me to see Grandma tomorrow."

"Is she?" His foster mom hadn't mentioned it when Shannon had picked him up this morning. "That will be nice."

Noah plopped onto the ground and leaned toward her, his soft curls tickling her neck as she slid her arm around him. "What if her memory is so bad that she doesn't know who I am?"

Oh, bud. How she wished she could assure him that would never happen. But with Mary Robinson's recent diagnosis of Alzheimer's, it was almost inevitable at some point. Shannon squeezed the boy and kissed the top of his head. "Even if your grandma's mind can't always remember, her heart will never forget you. How could anyone forget such a wonderful boy?"

Noah snuggled closer as the water lapped in and out.

Rocks skittered behind them, and a low growl rumbled in Lucky's throat, breaking the peace of the moment. The dog bounded toward the rocks and barked a few sharp warnings.

"Lucky!" Shannon's arm dropped from Noah's shoulders and she pivoted from her spot on the ground. "Wha—"

The question caught in her throat at the sight of a man standing not ten feet away, his hands held up as if a police officer had ordered him to surrender. "Whoa, boy."

Shannon scrambled to her feet. She should call Lucky off, but her tongue stuck to the roof of her mouth.

The man cleared his throat. "I'm sorry to interrupt, but—"

Lucky advanced a step, a deep growl breaking the man's speech. The guy took a step back.

Shannon shook herself from her stupor. "Lucky. Heel."

Her dog whipped his head around, big brown eyes mournful, but he eventually trotted to her side.

I'm so sorry. Why wouldn't the words come out of her mouth? Sure, she didn't have an affinity for chatting up strangers like her cousin Ashley, and she wasn't a take-charge type like her soon-to-be cousin Bella, but she *did* have common decency.

And yet, when a well-dressed man with gel-tousled brown hair, deep chocolate eyes, olive skin, and a straight Grecian nose looked at her, apparently Shannon's manners disappeared. All she could do was stand there like an idiot, blinking hard as if sand had settled into her eyelids. If only she had that excuse.

"Hi." Noah's voice sliced through the silence, causing Shannon to jump. Before she could remind Noah not to talk to strangers, the boy moved around her and toward the man. "My name's Noah."

"Hey, Noah. I'm Marshall." The guy's face lit up with a grin—and goodness, his five o'clock scruff made it hard to tell, but were those dimples on either side of his mouth?

Didn't matter that it was only seventy-something degrees out and Shannon wore shorts and a tank top. She was sweating. "Noah, let's not bother the poor man."

The boy's shoulders drooped at her words. He dragged his feet back toward the ocean, pulling Lucky along with him.

"He wasn't bothering me. I'm afraid I was unintentionally bothering you." Marshall stuck his hands into the pockets of his khaki shorts as he came to stand beside her. He wore a white button-up shirt rolled to his elbows, and his silver watch winked in the sunlight. Hints of some sort of exotic cologne filled the air between them.

He definitely was *not* from Walker Beach. She'd have remembered him for sure.

"You just surprised us. I didn't hear you coming at all." Shannon toed the sand before forcing herself to glance up into his eyes.

Her efforts were rewarded with another view of his dimples —yep, they were definitely there. "That's because I was here the whole time." He nodded at the rocks. "I got into town way too late to explore last night, so this morning I found myself wandering the beach and ended up in this little cove."

"And then we broke your peaceful retreat. I'm so sorry. And sorry about my dog. He doesn't act like that unless I'm being threatened." She winced. "Not that you were threatening us. He just misread the situation." Goodness, she was rambling.

But she didn't usually talk to guys she didn't know extremely well. Shannon Baker had never been *that* girl—bold, smooth, flirtatious. Not like Quinn.

Thankfully, Marshall ignored her blathering and offered an easy laugh. "No worries. That's the best kind of dog." He looked at Noah and Lucky, who were knee high splashing in the waves together. "He's really good with your son."

"Oh, he's n—" Shannon hesitated. "He's not my son ... yet."

"Yet?"

"I'm hoping to adopt him."

Her chest warmed at the thought of Noah moving into Bella's old room. In anticipation of her wedding next weekend, her former roommate had already moved into the house she and Shannon's cousin Ben were renting just a few miles away. Afterward, Shannon had made a whirlwind trip to Herman Hardware and purchased paint and a few decorations to get the room ready for Noah.

While she'd painted, she'd dreamed of their future. Of stargazing on summer nights and curling up by the fireplace reading stories during the winter. Of learning about sports for the first time because Noah was interested in baseball. Of giving the boy a sense of security he could count on for as long as she had the ability to provide it.

Shannon may not be a former NFL player like her brother, a business owner and town leader like her parents, or a hotshot marketing executive like her sister, but she *could* do this one meaningful thing with her life.

A tear slid down her cheek. She swiped it away.

"You all right?"

Oh, goodness. Right. Marshall was still here. What was she thinking, being so vulnerable in front of a stranger? "Y-yes. Sorry."

"Hey, don't apologize. I find your honesty refreshing."

Her eyes shot toward his again, but no, his serious gaze seemed just as genuine as his tone. Still . . . "We should leave you in peace."

"Eh, peace is overrated."

It was totally her imagination, but the way he looked at her —gaze narrowed but soft—made her feel like he saw something there worth knowing. But that was ridiculous. She wasn't anything special.

Besides, she'd misread a guy's interest before, and she wasn't making that mistake again. "I have a dinner to get ready for, and . . ." Her excuse trailed off.

"Ah, I see." A tease lit his eyes. "Hot date with your boyfriend?"

Sudden laughter burst from her throat. "Um, no." What would this guy say if he knew Shannon had never been on a date, much less had a boyfriend?

In the distance, seagulls swooped into the water, hunting for a late breakfast.

She pointed at Noah. "Besides my dad, brother, and a passel of cousins and uncles, *that* is the only man in my life."

As if sensing Shannon's attention, the kid looked up and

waved, a smile overtaking his face. Yes, they were going to be okay, even if the wait to be together was longer than she'd like. In the meantime, his social worker Miranda Shubert would make sure Noah was placed in good temporary foster homes once Florence moved. Shannon had already connected with Miranda several times, and she was the one who had suggested the adoption agency Shannon had chosen one town over.

Marshall squinted at Noah. "I mean, he's a little short, but I can see his appeal."

Shannon couldn't help but giggle. Oy, she must sound like a schoolgirl to this sophisticated guy, not a twenty-seven-year-old woman.

Marshall studied her for a beat before looking away and clearing his throat. "Hey, do you mind if I play a round of catch with Noah before you go?"

Really? He wasn't anxious to escape? "No, I don't mind."

"Great." He jogged toward Noah, holding up a hand and shouting something the wind carried away.

Moving back toward the rock where apparently Marshall had sat not twenty minutes ago, Shannon hunkered down to watch as Marshall and Noah tossed the football back and forth along the stretch of beach tucked away from the rest of the town. Lucky bounded between them, following the trajectory of the ball in an attempt to retrieve it.

A strange sensation slowly worked its way through Shannon's veins as she looked on. Something about the scene in front of her called, beckoned—demanded she stop sitting on the sidelines. Standing, Shannon brushed off the sand clinging to the backs of her legs and walked toward the guys.

Noah cheered as she approached Marshall. He lobbed the ball her way and she grimaced, squeezing her eyes shut as she held out her hands in an attempt to catch it. It gave a telltale *thwack* as it hit the ground.

"You know, it's a lot easier to catch when you can actually

see it coming." Marshall advanced, leaned down to pick up the ball, and slipped it into her fingers.

"You'd think I'd know that by now. My brother used to play football." She turned and lobbed the ball toward Noah—or attempted to, anyway. It fell pathetically short, giving Lucky the chance he'd been looking for to swoop in and steal it. He took off running toward the rocks, Noah shouting and hot on his trail. "Well, it's official. I'm going to be the worst boy mom ever."

"No way. I don't even know your name and I can tell you're going to be an amazing mother."

His declaration stole her breath.

It was dumb to be so affected by the confidence in a total stranger's tone, but still it meant something to her. Not even her parents had seemed so sure of her decision to adopt when she'd informed them about it a little over a week ago.

She hugged her waist. "Shannon." The word came out a whisper.

Marshall cocked his head, moved closer. "What?"

She tilted her chin upward—he had to be nearing six feet tall to her five five—licked her lips, and tried again. "My name is Shannon."

"That's a beautiful name for a beautiful woman."

She blinked, stepped back, shook herself from the trance. Because guys just didn't say things like that.

Well, they said them to her sister Quinn all the time.

But not to Shannon.

Clearly he was just an outrageous flirt.

His eyebrows scrunched together and he massaged the back of his neck. "Sorry, I really never say things like that. But today, I'm . . . not quite myself."

Oh.

Before Shannon could respond, Noah bounded back over, huffing, while a dejected Lucky followed. "Miss Shannon, can we try throwing again?"

"Of course, bud. I'll try to do better this time."

They spread out once more, forming a triangle. But it didn't matter how much she wanted to catch the ball—it slipped through her fingers every time. No wonder she'd nearly failed PE in high school.

Marshall jogged over. "I don't want to interfere, but would you like some pointers?"

"Yes, please."

And for the next fifteen minutes, he showed her the best way to position her hands to catch a ball above her waist and below it. She mixed them up several times, but then, miracle of miracles, she caught one.

Squealing, she held it up in triumph, and both Marshall and Noah ran toward her, whooping and celebrating with her. Noah threw his arms around her waist, and she caught Marshall's eye over his head. She mouth *Thank you*, and he just grinned in reply.

As soon as Noah let go, turning to run through the waves with Lucky once more, Marshall approached, holding up his hand for a high five. "Nice work."

"Thanks." She slapped his palm, and his fingers curled around hers for a moment longer than necessary.

A lump caught in her throat at the feel of her small hand in his larger one. When he dropped it, the tingle of his touch remained.

"I couldn't have done it without my awesome coach." Her lips tipped into a grin that grew serious far too quickly. "But really, thank you. You sure made a little boy's day. He hasn't had too many great ones lately and . . ." She sucked a breath between her teeth. Sudden exhaustion overtook her bones, and, frowning, Shannon sat down.

Marshall joined her, his strong forearms wrapped around his knees. "He's a great kid. And he clearly is enamored with you."

She ran her finger through the sand, at first drawing simple lines, then arcing out into a small picture. A house. A sun. "He doesn't know any better." Her attempt at a joke fell flat, as evidenced by Marshall's silence. Clearing her throat, she continued with the design.

"If you don't mind me asking, how do you know him?"

"I was his preschool teacher for two years. His grandma has had custody of him for a little longer than that, ever since his mom left to pursue an acting career in Los Angeles."

And then, as if she'd known this man forever, Shannon told him about her relationship with Noah, about Mary's mental decline, about how the final straw was her leaving Noah at the mall six weeks ago because she'd forgotten he was with her. "Social services removed him from the home, and Mary moved into a memory care facility. He's been with his neighbor ever since, but she and her family are moving out of state soon."

"So you're going to adopt him?"

"That's the plan. I was hoping I could get foster certification fast tracked since I already have fingerprint clearance and a background check due to my job. But there's just so much left in the process—an interview, adoption and fostering classes, psychiatric evaluation, home inspection—and each step takes time." Shannon added a woman to her sand picture. "So for a while, he'll have to live with someone else."

Marshall turned his face toward her, using his hand to block the sun that had slowly moved a bit farther westward. Whoa. It must be about two in the afternoon. How had three hours gone by so quickly? "Don't get me wrong, I think it's awesome. I'm just wondering why *you're* the one adopting him."

"If not me, then who?" She shrugged. "His social worker hasn't been able to get ahold of his mom, and he doesn't have any other family willing to take him. Walker Beach is an amazing community, but it's small. I'm afraid he'd eventually be sent to a town with more foster home options. But he should be able to stay near his grandma, the only family he has."

Shannon finished off her picture with a little boy holding hands with the woman. "Besides, I can't help but love him. And really, all you need is love to make a thing work, right?" Love—and a good dose of humility.

"Hmmm." A pause. "Hey, you're an artist."

She glanced up to find his eyes studying her silly picture. "Oh, that's . . . no. It's nothing."

"It's not nothing." He leaned in just a touch. "And neither are you."

If Shannon was made of ice, she'd be a puddle on the ground by now.

Sheesh. She needed to get control of her seesawing emotions. This was so silly. Marshall didn't know her. She didn't know him.

So how had his words stroked a hurting place in her heart that few even knew existed?

Shannon dusted off her hands and stood. "I had a really nice time with you, but I need to get Noah home."

Marshall pushed himself off the ground, then checked his watch. "Wow, it's later than I thought. I'd better get going as well."

They both stood there for a moment, looking at each other, the moment holding, suspended in time.

What was happening? Surely she was imagining this connection between them.

Shannon pulled her gaze from his. "Noah! Lucky! Time to go."

"Aw, man!" But despite his protest, the boy dragged his feet, hanging onto Lucky's collar as he trudged toward her.

She turned back to Marshall. "Thank you for teaching me to catch. And for listening while I talked your ear off."

There had been something so freeing about sharing with

someone she'd never see again. Because in a town the size of this one, everyone knew everyone else's business. And to them, Shannon Baker was merely the "shyest" member of the ginormous Baker clan, the daughter of the local pizza parlor owners, the younger sister of twins Tyler and Quinn.

The one always in her sister's vibrant and terrifying shadow.

But Marshall No Name from Who Knew Where—he only saw what she'd shown him. Whether he recognized it or not, he'd given her a gift. The ability, for a brief moment in time, to be more than she could be otherwise.

"It was my pleasure." He opened his mouth as if to say something, then closed it. Frowned. "Maybe I'll see you around?"

He wasn't going to ask for her number then. But what did she expect? She may have momentarily felt like Cinderella at the ball, but he was obviously someone else's Prince Charming.

Besides, she didn't have time for romance anyway. Her attention needed to stay focused on Noah's adoption. And, more immediately, on the Baker family reunion, since she was kind of in charge of the whole thing since her cousin Ashley had handed it over to her last month.

Shannon forced a smile. "Maybe."

"Would it be weird to ask for a hug?" And there was the adorably charming grin he'd flashed at her more than once today—the one that toasted her insides. "I mean, you did kind of tell me your life story."

Biting her lip, she studied him. "And yet I know almost nothing about you."

His features darkened for a moment, before it disappeared with a shrug. "Not much to tell. Although I will say . . . I felt more myself today than I have in a really long time. So thank you, Shannon."

Then he stepped forward and, after pausing to give her time to escape if she wanted to—she didn't—enveloped her in a hug. Now she could tell that his cologne smelled like cinnamon and some sort of flowers. Geraniums, maybe? Whatever it was, the combination was heady, as was the all-too-brief sensation of being in his arms.

Even if her proverbial midnight had finally arrived, *this* was what dreams were made of.

As Marshall stepped back, Shannon snagged Noah's hand in hers, whispered good-bye, tucked this perfect day away in her heart, and put on her game face.

Because dinner with her family—including Quinn—was just hours away.

And that was enough to spoil almost any fairytale.

BOOKS BY LINDSAY HARREL

Walker Beach Romance Series

All At Once (prequel novella)

All of You, Always

All Because of You

All I've Waited For

All You Need Is Love

Port Willis Series

The Secrets of Paper and Ink

Like a Winter Snow

Like a Christmas Dream

Standalones

The Joy of Falling

The Heart Between Us

One More Song to Sing

ABOUT THE AUTHOR

Lindsay Harrel is a lifelong book nerd who lives in Arizona with her young family and two golden retrievers in serious need of training. When she's not writing or chasing after her children, Lindsay enjoys making a fool of herself at Zumba, curling up with anything by Jane Austen, and savoring sour candy one piece at a time. Visit her at www.lindsayharrel.com.

facebook.com/lindsayharrel
instagram.com/lindsayharrelauthor

Walker Beach Romance Series

Book 3: All I've Waited For

Published by Blue Aster Press

Cover: Hillary Manton Lodge Design

Editing: Barbara Curtis